ENOUGH

MATT HEMINGWAY

This is a work of fiction. Names, characters, places, and incidents are products of the author's imagination or are used fictitiously and are not to be construed as real. Any resemblance to actual events, locations, organizations, or persons, living or dead, is entirely coincidental.

World Castle Publishing, LLC
Pensacola, Florida
Copyright © Matthew Hemingway 2019
Paperback ISBN: 9781950890385
eBook ISBN: 9781950890392
First Edition World Castle Publishing, LLC, August 26, 2019
http://www.worldcastlepublishing.com

Cover: Karen Fuller
Editor: Maxine Bringenberg

I know what a gun tastes like. I have never fired one, but I can tell you how the hard metal barrel feels when it slides across your teeth, and how the oil causes your entire mouth to salivate profusely. It's horrible. However, that kind of discomfort is not what's on your mind if you find yourself in that situation. The kind of pain that drives you to the moment that you know what a gun tastes like blots out all other pain, blots out everything.

CHAPTER 1

"Hey, fat ass."

"Does Maxy want a cookie?"

"You do know that eating isn't a full time job, right?"

One more. One more and I am going to snap. You would certainly think I would be used to this daily barrage of insults by now. This was just part of my routine. Wake up, brush my teeth, get dressed, and sit at the bus stop so I can be verbally abused for twenty minutes.

For a while I was trying to get to the bus stop at the last possible moment to avoid the whole scene, but I kept on missing the bus. Besides, running and thunder thighs really don't go together very well—the chafing is not worth it. Sometimes I underestimate my own chubbiness.

Today has been worse than most, because our bus driver was a newbie and he was running late. I hate it when the bus is late. It's like the kids in my school lose all self-control when they sense that they have five more minutes without adult supervision.

Either way, when that yellow wreck pulled up, I was relieved to have a change of scenery, even if the abuse was sure to continue. I waited for everyone else to get on first and then hoisted myself up the stairs, using the handicap rail for leverage. I thought I was going to get at least a moment or two of peace, until the new bus driver got a look at me.

"Whoa. You can sit by yourself if you want," blurted the driver. I think he was genuinely concerned about my comfort, or at least the comfort of the unlucky kid that would be stuck sitting with me. Unfortunately, his intentions didn't matter to Colin and his crew.

Colin Culler was my most recent, though certainly not my worst, problem. We had been going to school together since day one. He was the kind of kid that always had a group of thugs following him around. I can honestly say that I can't think of a single time that I saw him without his little posse. He pretty much ignored me from kindergarten until sixth grade. When middle school started, something changed. Colin seemed meaner, angrier. He had always been mean, but it had definitely intensified, and for some reason I became the target of this newfound rage. I really didn't know if his constant insults were an attempt to be funny to impress the half-wit gorillas that followed him around, or if he had brain damage. I will give him credit, though—at least his put downs were clever.

"Yeah, no need to double up there. Your seat is already handling a double load!" Colin shouted to his usual audience. I just smiled at the driver, thanked him, and told him I would figure it out. I could tell he felt bad about it and hadn't meant it that way. I was half expecting him to say something to those jerks, but he didn't. He just shot them a look. Maybe he was just as afraid of them as I was. Most adults talk a good game, but they really don't know how to handle these situations any better than we do.

I turned sideways and shuffled down the slippery center aisle of the bus until I reached a seat near the middle. I usually try to sit in this area for a couple of reasons. #1- All the jerks sit in the back of the bus, and #2- If I sit in the front I will hear about it when I get off the bus for being a "baby" that needs to be near the bus driver. So I settle in the middle. There is still a chance that both things could happen, but my odds improve significantly. With the right seat, some days I can even get a little nap in before the torture of exiting the bus begins.

Today the odds were not in my favor.

As I scanned the middle section of the bus I noticed that the only seat available was next to Michael Dryden. I know it sounds hypocritical, but there was no way I was sitting next to that kid. He stank. I know I have my own issues, but mine don't wash off—his do. Life is tough enough when you take care of the things you can control. I have no sympathy for people that choose not to make things as comfortable as possible for themselves. I know what you're thinking; "Then put down the pizza, chubby." It's not that simple. I didn't eat because I loved food—I ate because I hated myself. It's a long story. Don't worry, I will get to it eventually.

As I slid past Michael's seat he scooched over to make room for me, but I just rolled my eyes and kept moving. His eyes actually looked red, as if he'd been rubbing at them or something. Probably had pink eye. I felt kind of bad, but the only thing more tempting for a bully than an easy target was two easy targets. I wasn't about to make this any more convenient for them if I could help it.

I spun around to peek back at the seats towards the front of the bus. They were all taken. I looked down at Michael again, with his dirty Tigers sweatshirt and torn jeans. I was just about to give up and have a seat when, I swear, I saw a bug jump out of his hair. Now, that bug could have just been casually passing through and not have come from Michael in the first place—still, I wasn't taking any chances. I had no choice. I had to move to the back of the bus.

Now, any kid that has ever ridden the bus knows there is definitely a pecking order that determines where you can sit. It is a lot like a wolfpack. The sick and frail tend to stay near the driver for protection. The alpha wolves gravitate towards the back, and all the wanna-be's find a spot in the middle that is within striking distance of the big dogs, but still close enough to the front to get back to safety when necessary.

I think I would rather be under the bus than in the back. I say this because when a "wolf" steps out of their assigned location in the pack, there are usually consequences.

Colin and his cronies wasted no time letting me know that I was in unfriendly territory.

"Quick! Hide your lunches!"

"Oh no! The bus is going to pop a wheelie!"

"Is that an eclipse or is Max blocking the sun?"

Mind you, none of these insults were new to me. I could have added a dozen more on my own. Today shouldn't have been any different than every other miserable day of my pathetic life, but it did feel different somehow. For some reason I was just a little more sensitive. I had become so used to hearing these things about myself that I stopped taking them personally. I just kind of figured that every overweight kid went through this. But for some reason, those verbal razor blades dug a little deeper today. I know I should have just turned and headed back the way I came, but I couldn't. I just stood there, staring at them. I must have looked like a total moron. I wanted to speak — I had so many words right on the tip of my tongue.

"Got a problem, tubby?" Colin sneered at me. He had gotten up from his seat and was now inches from my face. "Spit it out." His crew was cheering him on all around us. They wanted a fight.

Usually at this point in a story the reader expects to hear about how the bullied young man rises above his tormentors, lashes out at them by telling the bullies how badly they have hurt him, and the bullies finally see the light and are remorseful for the way they've treated him all those years. The story ends with the victim and victimizer walking off arm in arm as new friends to play ball together.

That would have been nice. Unfortunately, my life is not a novel and it certainly doesn't have a happy ending. I did not lash out. There was no ball game. Instead I did the worst thing

a kid in my situation could do.
  I cried.

CHAPTER 2

The blood was in the water and the sharks were circling. I am not sure exactly how to describe what happened that morning. I am usually not a very emotional kid, but it was as if a pipe inside of me broke. Tears and snot and sniffles were flowing out of me faster than I could suck them back in. I had been through this exact scenario dozens of times and not cried. Apparently, this time was one too many.

I stood in the aisle and twisted my face up, desperately trying to prevent myself from completely losing it in front of the entire bus. I could feel it coming, but couldn't do anything to stop it. I pulled my hoodie up over my face and frantically tried to dry my eyes, but I couldn't keep up. After several moments of pure panic, I gave up and slumped into the nearest seat with my face buried in my hands. The girl already occupying that seat shrieked as she nearly climbed the wall of the bus to get away from me. I lost my balance and rolled backwards, pinning her against the window. That poor little thing was Mariah Hayward. A few years down the road she actually became the closest thing I ever had to a real friend—but at the moment, she was Colin Culler's girlfriend.

Colin immediately lunged at me. Without a moment's hesitation he leapt into the air and came down with the heel of his right foot square in the middle of my chest. The wind exited my lungs in a violent whoosh as he simultaneously grabbed my hair with both hands and pulled me off of innocent little Mariah. Despite all the pain I was in, I can still remember feeling genuinely bad for her. She didn't ask to have a blubbering elephant sit on her that day. While she had every right to be angry with me, I swear she was just as angry with Colin.

"The big idiot didn't mean it," she yelled at Colin as she pushed past him and stepped over me on her way toward the front of the bus. Colin started to go after her, but stopped to drive the heel of his other foot into the side of my head before returning to his original seat. I guess I was an easier fight than his girlfriend was at that moment.

"Knock it off and sit down," the new bus driver screamed from the front. "If I have to stop this bus we are all going to be late!" This comment received a round of rowdy cheers from the rest of the bus.

I lay on the floor of that bus for another ten minutes, without a single soul even taking a second to see if I was okay. A couple of the younger kids twisted around in their seats and stared at me, but nobody got up. People think that being completely by themselves is the loneliest feeling in the world. I can tell you, without a doubt, that loneliness has nothing to do with the number of people near you. I was surrounded by sixty classmates on that bus, and had never felt more alone.

A few blocks from school my tears finally stopped and I pulled myself up into a sitting position. I think the only feeling worse than embarrassing yourself in front of a bunch of people is the feeling you get immediately after you have embarrassed yourself in front of a bunch of people. In the heat of the moment, it makes sense to have snot and tears running down your face. After that moment has passed, it's just pathetic.

I wiped my face on the sleeve of my hoodie. I always wear a hoodie — they are like camouflage for a fat kid. I would have to wash it off when I arrived at school, but that wasn't important at the moment. All I wanted to do was get off the bus.

I could already hear Colin and his followers talking about how they were going to reenact the whole scene for the kids that weren't lucky enough to be on bus #50 that fine October morning. My stomach flipped. How much more could a kid take? I had to get out of there. Should I pretend to be throwing up? No, just more eating jokes. Should I stand up and hit one of them? Not unless I wanted to get my butt kicked some more.

Instead, I did what I always do—I sat there and took it. I would love to tell you how ridiculous all of the screaming, crying, and sniffling during their role playing was. Unfortunately, I think they pretty much nailed it.

Finally, the bus pulled to a screeching, bone rattling halt in front of Lincoln Middle School. I gathered my things, wiped my face again, and waited for everyone else to leave the bus first. Colin, Anthony, and the rest still had enough energy left to puff out their cheeks, put their arms out to their sides as if they were obese, and waddle past me on their way out. It didn't matter. I was numb at that point. After they passed, I stood and shuffled off the bus, past the new bus driver. He looked down and pretended to be busy scribbling on a clipboard to avoid eye contact with me. I am almost positive he could see everything that happened that day in his huge mirror, yet he did nothing. I can't say that I really blame him. I try to ignore what I see in the mirror, too.

CHAPTER 3

Before we continue with Yet-Another-Miserable-Day-in-the-Life-of-Max Hefler, I think there is some background information you need to know. Otherwise the choices I made at the end of this day might not make a whole lot of sense. Not that the choices I made that day could ever make sense. Those choices can be explained.

At the time of this particular day of my life I am fourteen years old and an eighth grader at Lincoln Middle School. I hate this place. I honestly would rather be anywhere else in the world than here. Just in case you couldn't tell already, I do have a wee bit of an eating problem. I am about 5'9" tall, and tip the scales at about 230 pounds. You could say that I am a "big boned" young man, or as my doctor preferred to call me, "morbidly obese."

I have been big for as long as I can remember. I always knew I was different, but I wasn't aware that being big was necessarily a bad thing until third grade. Around that time a couple of kids in my class started calling me "Husky." At first I thought it was a pretty cool nickname. I found a picture of a husky, the dog, on a website. It looked like a wolf, and they were known for their amazing strength. Cool. The fact that these kids usually giggled after they said it never really dawned on me until later. This realization came when my mom and I were shopping at Sears for some pants—I had outgrown my old ones. Mom had a job at the time, so I was actually going to be able to get a new pair instead of settling for something from the second-hand store across town.

We entered the building, and I immediately headed for the boys' section.

"Nope. Over here," my mom called out. "Those aren't going to work anymore, my growing boy. We need to check out the husky section."

"Awesome," I said. *A husky section!* I thought I was going to get some cool looking pants that will reflect the fierce personality and muscle that came with my new nickname. I walked out of the boy's section and moved to where the Husky clothes were kept. I was feeling good until I looked up and saw the store sign hanging over some very wide shirts. It read, "Husky — For the Big Kid on the Block." Below it was a fat kid wearing very baggy pants and a huge hoodie. I am sure he would have been just as tall laying on his back as he was standing up. He also looked a lot like me. That's when it hit me — they weren't calling me Husky because of my rugged good looks or superhuman strength. They were calling me that because I was just like the kid on the sign. If you could actually hear joy leaving a person's body, everyone in Sears that day would have gone deaf. From that moment on I don't think I ever walked into school without thinking about my weight.

The sad thing is, I don't really enjoy eating. You would think getting to that point must have been at least a little fun. But no, that hadn't been the case at all. I did most of my eating alone, behind closed doors. I did this for a couple of reasons. First, I didn't want to hear about how fat I was getting, which inevitably happened if I ate in public. I am not proud of my weight, but it is what it is. You'd be surprised how much unsolicited advice gets thrown at a fourteen-year-old who is double fisting hot dogs in the mall food court.

I actually had a lady approach me and my mom at McDonald's once and point at my Double Quarter Pounder with Cheese and say, "You know, there are a lot of calories in one of those things." She looked like she was in her late thirties. She was very well dressed, and was flanked on both sides by two kids who looked as if they'd just stepped out of a Hollister billboard. Her husband stood about ten feet behind her, looking slightly embarrassed.

I stopped mid-bite and looked at my mom. I was shocked into silence. I could tell by the twinkle in her eye she was about to have some fun with this lady. Her eyes widened as she feigned surprise. She dramatically swatted the burger out of my hand, onto the table, and said, "Whew. That was a close one. Thank you, ma'am. If he's not careful he may get big. I thought that was salad. You saved my baby's life!" At that point we both cracked up. The smug look evaporated from the lady's face, and she gave us a grunt of disapproval and moved on. I love my mom.

She and I are actually quite a bit alike. We definitely have the same sense of humor. I think most people would categorize it as "childish," but we really don't care. I think that's what makes her so much fun to be around. She can find something funny in almost any situation.

One of our favorite past-times is people watching. The best place to do this is Walmart, easily. Once we spent an hour sitting on the bench outside of the Photoshop, adding our own dialogue to the people walking by. While we were checking out the locals, or Walmartians as we call them, a very small woman with a monstrous tattoo of a butterfly on her shoulder came plowing past us, dragging two little kids by the hands. She looked angry, as if the kids were misbehaving or something. My mom leaned in towards me, gave her best hillbilly accent, and said, "Hurry up, Clem and Daisy.

That there butterfly is gainin' on us. Run for tha' trailer!"

I chimed in with an accent of my own and said, "It's too late. It's got Momma. Save yourself!" We almost fell out of our seats laughing so hard. There is never a dull moment when we are together.

The other reason I eat so much is a lot deeper and harder to understand. I am not sure I completely understand it myself. On the daytime TV shows my mom watches, they call it, "Eating Your Feelings," whatever that means. One big bald guy with a mustache, Dr. Something or Other, once told a kid like me, "You ain't gonna find what makes you happy at the bottom of that bag of cookies, son." He's right. I should know—I've been to the bottom of a few bags of cookies. They say it's easier to keep chewing than to think about why you feel the way you do. If that's true, then I must have a hell of a lot of feelings inside of me.

CHAPTER 4

You should also probably know that I am not really a "people person." Since I had been a student at Lincoln I'd had two full conversations with an adult. Exactly two. I am not saying the adults at Lincoln are uncaring or mean—not at all. We have some really nice teachers and counselors. The truth is I did everything I could to avoid them. I tried the talking thing. It really didn't do me much good. My life is what it is. I didn't see the point in talking it to death. If I have something important to say, I say it. Otherwise I keep my mouth shut. It's actually a little bit scary when I think about how easy it is for a kid to go unnoticed by so many people for so long.

The first conversation came when my sixth-grade teacher, Mrs. Brantley, called me out into the hallway during silent reading time. "Maxwell, someone needs to speak with you." At first I didn't even react, because no one calls me Maxwell, and because I couldn't remember the last time Mrs. B used my first name. I actually looked around like I expected someone else to stand up. This drew a few snickers from my classmates, when I realized she was talking about me and jumped to my feet. Everyone was terrified of Mrs. B. She was the type of teacher you just assumed went home and beat someone—a dog, her husband, somebody.

Most teachers called me Hefler, or Big Guy. I guess I am not all that memorable, and I kind of like it that way. Under the radar is the place to be, in my humble opinion. I stood up from my desk and walked towards the door. Unfortunately, my desk must not have wanted me to leave and decided to hold onto my hips and waist as I stood. The racket it made was horrible—metal on metal. I grunted as I pushed the desk down. It made a horrible banging sound as it hit the desk behind me. I wanted to disappear. A couple of girls in class shrieked, and one boy pretended the ground was shaking. I was mortified. Every eye in the room was looking at me. I could feel my face getting redder by the second.

Instinctively, I turned to Mrs. Brantley, expecting her to rip into my classmates for being so cruel. Unfortunately, I saw something completely different on her face than what I expected. Amusement. I didn't get it at first. I expected to see the rage she usually released when there was any disruption in her room. Then I realized what was going on. She was laughing at me, too. She had her right hand covering her mouth, but there was no doubt that her eyes were smiling. Now, this wasn't the first time I was betrayed by an adult (Like I said, I will get to that later) but it was definitely hard to wrap my head around. Up to this point of 6th grade it had kind of been Mrs. Brantley versus the class. It was as close as I'd felt to being a part of a team in a long time. But that moment changed everything. She was on their side, and I wasn't. I had gone from being one of thirty, to just one. Alone. Worst of all, the other team had a teacher on their side.

After the shock of what was happening

passed, I continued into the hallway to have that conversation. Seated at a small table in the hall was a pretty woman with short red hair, wearing a blue pantsuit. It has always cracked me up when adults sit on kid-sized furniture. It reminds me of when they make elephants stand on those little stools at the circus. She was staring intently at a couple of pieces of paper when she peeked over the top of them and smiled at me. It was one of those smiles where I didn't know if I should smile back or check to see if my wallet was gone. I didn't completely trust her. I honestly couldn't tell you why.

"Hello, Maxwell. My name is Mrs. Hendricks. I was hoping we could talk for a minute."

She motioned towards an empty chair and I very carefully sat down, and then stood back up, and then down again. I wanted to avoid a repeat of what just happened in class. Mrs. Hendricks gave me a quizzical look, yet said nothing. She just gave me a little smirk like she was used to this sort of behavior, and started with the interrogation.

"I have a couple of questions to ask you,

Maxwell, and I want you to answer them as honestly as you can." I didn't like where this was going. Anytime an adult tells you they want you to be honest, it usually means that you have good reason not to be. I had no idea what she was going to ask, but my guard was now up.

"Okay."

"Who do you live with, Max?"

"My mom and her boyfriend." This was easy.

"What is this boyfriend's name, and how long have you lived with him?"

"Sam. He moved into our apartment right after Halloween," I replied. All true so far. Although Mom had only been dating him for a couple of weeks, she insisted that he was going to move in because he had been evicted from his place. I kind of saw it coming, because Mom was laid off. I am sure a roommate helps with the rent, but he definitely wouldn't have been my first choice. In fact, he would not have made the top twenty.

Sam was kind of a small guy, yet he tried to make himself look bigger than he was by increasing his volume. He. Never. Shut. Up. On top of that, he always reeked of cigars, cheap cologne, and stupidity.

"How do you and Sam get along?"

"Okay, I guess." Complete lie. Sam and I hated each other. He was always grabbing at my mom and kissing her in front of me. I could tell it made her uncomfortable, too. Not even that kept him from doing it. It was almost like he was trying to bait me into saying something to him.

Sometimes at night I could hear them fighting. I was usually not part of the argument, but every once in a while I heard the words "chubby," "fat boy," or "lard-ass" thrown around, and I knew he was talking about me. I felt bad for Mom during these fights. It can't be easy having a kid like me and trying to find a boyfriend. She deserved better than Sam, but who wants a girlfriend with a loser son? I usually just stuck to my room when he was around. As you have probably already figured out, I don't do well with confrontation.

"Has he ever done or said anything that made you feel uncomfortable?" asked Mrs. Hendricks.

"No, ma'am. Nothing." I knew what she was getting at. Sam was a lot of horrible things, but a pervert wasn't one of them. I can usually see those guys coming from a mile away. I would be lying if I told you I wasn't tempted at that moment to say he had done something inappropriate, so I could watch his sorry butt get locked up forever. Lucky for him, my mother raised me better than that.

"Are you sure? Anything you tell me will be just between us, sweetheart." That is one of my all-time favorite adult lies. The truth would sound more like, "Anything you tell me is between you, me, and any other adult that I happen to want to have a conversation with in the near future." They really must think we are stupid.

"Positive," I replied.

Mrs. Hendricks thanked me and walked me back into the room. Mrs. B stepped out into the hall with her for a moment before returning to class and telling us to get our math books out. For the rest of the day I kept on catching her looking at me with a strange expression on her face, almost like she felt sorry for me. I just wasn't sure if she felt that way because she'd laughed at me or because she thought my home life sucked.

That was the last I heard about the situation until about a year later. By this time my mother had left Sam. He slapped her hard enough to bruise her left cheek when he came home drunk and angry after losing our rent money playing cards with his loser buddies. I hid in my room and pretended to be asleep—not one of my prouder moments. I had no idea what to do. I just squeezed my eyes shut tight and prayed.

One night I overheard Mom telling a neighbor lady about how her ex-boyfriend was in jail because they discovered that he'd done some really bad things to some of his other girlfriends and their kids. Maybe my "pervert detector" wasn't as strong as I thought it was. I never asked her about it because I didn't want to get in trouble for listening to her conversation. That was the only time in my life I was ever glad someone hit my mother.

Chapter 5

The second real conversation I had with an adult at Lincoln Middle School was a lot less formal. It was with Mr. Mark, our custodian. He was a huge, bulging man who breathed way too heavily as he walked down the hall. He had a deep accent that sounded like it followed him up from somewhere down south, and a not-so-great grasp of basic grammar when he spoke. Otherwise, he didn't draw much attention to himself. He usually just kind of blended into the background.

It was a pretty typical Tuesday morning, and I was hiding behind the door to the janitor's supply closet waiting for my latest tormentors to pass by before heading to class. I was peeking around the edge of the door when I was surprised to hear a voice behind me.

"What you so scared of, big boy? They's gonna bite you or somethin'?" Mr. Mark asked between bites of the peanut-butter and jelly sandwich he was devouring while sitting on an overturned mop bucket. "You'se can't hide forever."

"I am not hiding," I snarled back at him over my shoulder. Total lie. Of course I was hiding.

"Sure you are. You'se actin' like a big baby. Them boys ain't nothin' to be scared of. You start hidin' from people like that now, you'se gonna be hidin' fo' the rest of your life. Man up and get your big ass out there. They ain't nothin' special."

I wasn't sure where this conversation was going, but it was already beginning to piss me off. I may be fat, but I am definitely not stupid, and I wasn't going to let this janitor tell me how to live my life. Looking back on it now, I probably should have taken his advice.

"Screw you," I mumbled under my breath.

"That's more like it!" Mr. Mark cackled as bits of bread and grape jelly rolled down his chin. "Now you'se needs to say it to them!"

Whatever. I peeked down the hallway one more time to make sure that the coast was clear. The hallway was now almost deserted, and I decided it was safe enough to venture out. Besides, I'd heard enough of Mr. Mark's crap for one day.

I was just about to leave when he spoke up again. This time his voice was calmer, firmer, more serious.

"Hey, look, big boy. I ain't trying to be your daddy or nuthin. It's just that I knew a boy 'lot like you once. Long time ago. He was scared, too. He let boys like 'dem get under his skin. He was hurt'n real bad, but didn't do nuthin 'bout it."

I could see where he was going with this one. Adults are always trying to pass off their own sob stories as, "Someone I knew once" life lessons. I'd heard enough of these fairytales to see one coming.

"Let me guess—you are that boy, and you stood up to the bullies and now you get to have *all* of this," I said sarcastically, as I swept my right arm in a wide arc around the janitorial closet. I instantly felt bad. I guess I can be a real jerk sometimes, too.

If Mr. Mark was insulted, he didn't show it. In fact, his face softened a bit and he smiled a little as he said, "Nope. Wasn't me, but might as well have been. Poor boy didn't know what to do. I wish I woulda given him a kick in the pants. Too late now."

Okay. I admit it. He had me curious. "Is 'this boy' okay now?" I asked, using air quotes to show him that I still wasn't buying his alter ego completely.

"I likes to think he is. Been a long time...." Mr. Mark trailed off. His mind seemed to be somewhere else as he closed his eyes and leaned forward, putting his elbows on his knees. He sat like that for a hot second before he stood up suddenly, turned his back to me, and flipped his mop bucket back over. Without facing me again, he said, "Now get yo' butt to class. Got work to do. No more hidin'. You hear me, boy?"

I didn't answer him. Instead, I slipped back into the hall and closed the door behind me. I knew Mr. Mark was right. I couldn't hide forever, even though it sure seemed like my best option at that moment.

CHAPTER 6

That conversation with Mr. Mark was running through my head as I made my way up the front stairs of the school, through the double doors, and headed toward my locker. This was not my favorite part of the day. I really don't have any friends, so any interactions I have are usually not pleasant.

I moved through the hall with amazing agility for a big guy. When you walk with your head down trying to avoid all eye contact on a daily basis, you develop an almost bat-like sonar to avoid things you can't, or don't want to, see.

I fumbled with my lock for a couple of seconds before finally getting it opened. The days of sixth grade anxiety over opening a combination lock were over, although sometimes it still took me a couple of tries. I squeezed my book bag inside, grabbed my planner, a pencil, and slammed my locker shut. I had Mr. Davis for first hour English. I had to hustle because his room was clear across the school. It was one of the few classes I never wanted to be late for.

I actually feel that way about most classes. It's usually because I don't want detention, or worse yet, to have everyone's attention on me as I come into the room. Sometimes I could just slip in and sit down, but other times the fat jokes would start flying. Of course, a fat kid couldn't be late because he had trouble with his lock, or he forgot something in his last class, or he was dropped off late. No way. If a fat kid is late for class it's because his belly got stuck in his locker or there was an All-You-Can-Eat Buffet somewhere. Or my all-time favorite, he had to wait for someone to grease him up so they could squeeze him through the front door. Typical middle school humor.

No, the reason I never wanted to be late for Mr. Davis's class was because you never knew what was going to happen in his room.

He was the kind of teacher who could leave you hyperventilating and holding your stomach from laughing so much during a lesson about quotation marks. He always seemed to have a fresh way of looking at things, and didn't seem to care what anyone else thought about it, except us. I know every teacher tells you they care, but he really seemed to mean it. When Mr. Davis asked you how you were doing, it wasn't immediately followed with a half-hearted pat on the shoulder and quick dismissal. He actually looked at you as if he was waiting for an answer. It catches a lot of kids off guard at first. He shows up at sporting events, band concerts, school plays, and anywhere else you might find middle schoolers.

I even saw him shopping at the Salvation Army store one day. My mom and I were regulars there since she lost her job at the auto parts plant, but to see a teacher there, that was weird. At first I thought he must have a gambling or drinking problem and couldn't afford nice things. That's usually the story when you see grown men in my neighborhood shopping at the thrift stores.

I watched him for a minute from behind a rack of smelly-old-lady winter coats. It took me a moment to realize he was looking through a rack of kid's clothes. He was not a big man, but I didn't think he was buying a small Abercrombie hoodie for himself. I never said anything to him that day and never brought it up at school, but I did notice Michael Dryden was wearing almost the exact same hoodie a couple of days later. For a little while he even smelled okay enough to sit next to on the bus. You get the picture. Mr. Davis was that kind of guy.

CHAPTER 7

I hurried into the classroom, getting my Mr. D fist bump and a smile on my way through the door, and shimmied sideways down the aisle to my seat. This was one of the very few places in Lincoln Middle School, or anywhere else for that matter, that I truly felt safe.

However, nowhere is ever completely safe in middle school. I was walking to my seat when a girl, who we'll call Abby (because that's her name and I hate her and I don't care if you know her real name), stuck out her foot and tripped me. I could see the whole thing coming as if it was in slow motion. Abby glanced at the girl across the aisle from her, smiled, looked back straight ahead, and shot her skinny little chicken leg out in front of me.

Although I could see it all happening, when you are 230 lbs., stopping on a dime is not one of your strong suits. I tried to step over her but didn't make it. I lifted my foot a little higher and tried to skip over this sudden obstacle. My front foot cleared her by a good six inches — my back foot, not so much. My toes caught her shin and I flopped over on my back, right in the middle of the row, with an audible grunt as I hit the floor. I must have looked like a humpback whale trying to pole vault.

I laid there for a second staring at the ceiling, waiting for the eruption of laughter. Mr. Davis rushed over from his post at the front door to see if I was okay.

"You all right, Max? What happened?"

"Yeah, I'm okay," I grunted while struggling to get to a sitting position. Mr. D put an arm behind my back and helped me up. "Need to watch where I am going," I mumbled.

It was pretty obvious to everyone in the room that this wasn't an accident. I fully expected Mr. D to either, A-ignore it and move on, or B-scream at Abby. That's why I was so caught off guard by what happened next. He turned away from me and put a hand on Abby's shoulder.

"Abby, are you okay?" Mr. D asked in a very concerned, sweet voice, that if taken out of context, could have easily been mistaken as genuine.

"Um, yeah. I didn't fall on my face," replied Abby as she shared a sarcastic smile with her friend and rolled her eyes.

"I know, but you must be traumatized by what just happened. I mean, you were right there when this klutz nearly fell on you. Do you need ice? A cold glass of water?" gushed Mr. Davis. I was so confused. I thought he was going to help me, not take care of the person that put me there in the first place.

Abby was beginning to look very uncomfortable. I don't think any part of her master plan had included drawing this much attention to herself. The plan was to shine the spotlight on my fat behind as I lay on the floor. She managed a quiet, "No thank you," as she tried to look busy shuffling papers on her desk.

"Oh, but please, at least sit in my chair. I can't imagine the mental anguish you are dealing with right now." He wasn't letting up. At this point it was beginning to dawn on me, and the rest of the class, that Mr. D was trying to make a point, and an example, out of Abby. "Max, go get my swivel chair from behind my desk. Hurry up. Stop being so selfish. Think about poor Abby here."

I could see a little twinkle in his eye, but short of a wink, when he looked away from Abby and back at me. I waddled as quickly as I could up to his desk, and came whipping back down the aisle with his comfy looking chair. Mr. D attempted to coax Abby out of her desk.

Abby was really squirming now. She was visibly upset. She quickly stood, grabbed the chair, and spun it back around so that it was now facing me. "I'm okay, really. Maybe Max could use the chair. He's the one who fell down."

Mr. Davis intercepted the chair and made a hand motion, indicating that he wanted to me sit. "Wow. That is so generous of you, Abby. It truly warms my heart to see students looking out for each other. Eighth grade is hard enough when you have a ton of help. Doing it alone is damn near impossible. Take a seat, Max," Mr.

D said.

I plopped down with a huge smile on my face. I wasn't sure where he was going with all of this, but I was loving every second of it.

"Everyone, please get out your grammar notebooks and get ready to take a few notes about similes and metaphors," Mr. Davis instructed as he strode back toward the front of the room. "Oh, Abby. Mr. Hefler looks like he has a swollen wrist from his little tumble. Would you mind taking notes for him as well?"

I expected a dirty look, the finger, something from Abby. Instead she just nodded and pulled out another sheet of paper. For the rest of class I sat in that big cozy chair and watched her take my notes as Mr. Davis taught us about figurative language. I kept waiting for something bad to happen. Things rarely continued going this well for me for very long.

After class, Abby came up to me and handed me my notes. She didn't say a word. She did look up for a second and make eye contact. I could see from the look on her face she was sorry, but not sorry enough to say it in front of her friends. It wasn't a complete victory, but I take what I can get.

Abby never gave me or anyone else much more trouble while in Mr. D's room. She wasn't necessarily nice, but she didn't go out of her way to be mean anymore either. I think Abby is one of those types of bullies that had just never really thought about how it makes other people feel. Mr. D made her do that, and I think something clicked inside of her.

From that moment forward I never had to worry about being picked on in Mr. Davis's class. That day he made a couple of things very clear. The first thing a lot of teachers do right — he showed us bullying would not be ignored in his room. However, it was the second part that I don't think I will ever forget. Most teachers would have screamed at Abby and sent her to the office. She would then have another reason to target me, and the whole thing would start over again. Mr. D didn't do that. He tried to make her feel what I was feeling, embarrassment. He never demanded that she do anything as far as an apology was concerned. He simply made her realize what it felt like to be singled out, and gave her the opportunity to make it better.

Sometimes I think that is all anybody needs, a chance to make things better.

CHAPTER 8

"Hold up, Max," Mr. Davis whispered to me as I was about to leave the room and head to my least favorite part of my day — gym class. "You really okay?" he asked.

"Yeah. It wasn't as bad as it looked. Thanks for helping me out with her," I replied, nodding toward Abby.

"No need to thank me. She's not all bad. You let me know if anything else happens, okay?"

"Sure thing, Mr. D," I answered. Wow. My third full conversation with an adult.

Before I left, Mr. Davis wrote me a pass to P.E. class. He knew I was going to be late because of our conversation. I took my sweet time getting there, because I absolutely hate P.E. class. Our teacher, Mr. Drummond, is a complete tool. He walks around with his chest stuck out like he doesn't realize that he already looks like five pounds of crap in a two-pound bag stuffed into those running suits he wears all the time.

Besides, tossing me a ball and telling me to play is about the equivalent of giving a hippopotamus a pair of hummingbird wings and telling it to fly. He can try all he wants—it ain't happening.

I was happy at least I wasn't going to have to dress in front of the other guys. I absolutely hate having to do that. The locker room might be the only place I like less than the bus. If I have to listen to one more stupid joke about not being able to see my "stuff," I swear I am going to lose it.

I opened the locker room door and shuffled past the first bank of lockers, heading to the second row. I had planned on staying put for a few minutes and wasting as much time as possible, since I already had a pass from Mr. Davis that he forgot to write a time on.

I turned the corner and realized I wasn't alone. My breath caught in my throat and I nearly screamed. It took me a few seconds to wrap my brain around what I was seeing. Standing with his back to me, about twenty feet away, was Colin Culler. He was just getting ready to pull up the sweatpants he always wore for gym class when I saw it.

Colin's legs looked like someone had taken a baseball bat to them. They were black and purple from his knees up to his hips. From the knees down it was even worse. He had dried blood crusted up on his shins, and I think I even saw some burn marks on his left calf.

I was shocked. It was as if all the things I secretly had wished would happen to Colin actually did happen. I was also shocked that I wasn't happy about it. This was my mortal enemy. He had embarrassed, hurt, humiliated, and punished me in every way possible. He made my life a living hell. I should have been doing cartwheels. But I didn't (and couldn't if I wanted to). Instead, I felt horribly guilty for ever wishing anything bad would happen to him. In fact, for the second time that day, I started to cry.

The tears ran down my cheeks in silence as

I watched Colin get dressed. It just occurred to me that I had never actually seen him do this before. Now that I thought about it, he was always the last one out of, and into, the locker room. I guess we both had a good reason to avoid the locker room.

Apparently I was taking all of this even harder than I thought, because a snort escaped me as I stood there sniffling in disbelief. Colin whirled around on his heels. He glared at me with eyes the size of the bruises on his legs. Almost instantly his bewildered look turned into one of pure hatred and rage.

"What the hell are you looking at, fat boy? You trying to steal a peek at me while my pants are down? I knew you were fat. I didn't know you a perv, too."

I wasn't even upset by Colin's words. I could completely understand why he said them. Any anger I could have had at that moment was totally buried by pity and curiosity.

"What happened to your legs?" I barely whispered.

"Mind your own business," Colin half shouted, half growled at me. I thought about getting out of there, but I couldn't. I don't know why, but I had to stay. It was like someone else had control of my legs.

"What happened?" I repeated.

"Get the hell out of here, fat boy!" he screeched as he pointed toward the door. Colin's eyes were now filling with tears, and his bottom lip trembled as he spoke. I knew that I was getting dangerously close to being pummeled. There was no one around to stop it once it got started. Still, something kept me from running. I had to know.

"No. Tell me what happened." The words narrowly escaped my lips before I could close my mouth. This was the breaking point. I was either going to get punched in the face or he was going to tell me. There really wasn't any other choice. He certainly wasn't going to run out into the gym in that condition. He had a reputation to think about.

Colin's face curled into a ball of anger and he clenched his fists. He lunged towards me with both of his hands raised above his head. His face was inches away from mine. I could smell his sour breath and feel a mist of perspiration from his sweaty forehead land on my cheek. I instinctively closed my eyes and winced, waiting for the blow. But it never came. I opened my eyes to find Colin sitting on the floor, legs splayed out, back against the lockers. He was now sobbing so uncontrollably that he couldn't seem to catch his breath. I sat on the bench across from him and waited for whatever was going to come next. I don't know why I was still in that locker room. It just felt like I SHOULD be there, if that makes any sense.

The few seconds that we sat in awkward silence felt like hours. Finally, Colin said, "My dad."

At first I was confused. I thought he was asking for his dad. I started to get up to try and find someone to call his dad when it hit me. He was telling me what happened. I stopped walking and turned back to face him.

"Your dad did that to you?" I asked. It must not have sounded like I meant it to, because my question infuriated Colin all over again.

"At least I have a dad to hit me!" Colin screamed. He was obviously still very frustrated, and he was right. My dad hadn't been around in a very long time. There was a good reason for that, but I wasn't in the mood to argue about it. Later on, I couldn't help but wonder how he knew about my dad. I never spoke to him, or anybody else in school, about it.

"Why did he do it?"

"Because I jumped on him," Colin answered.

"Why'd you jump on him?" It was like my mouth was saying these things before I could stop it.

"Because my mom stopped moving," he replied. He took a deep breath to compose himself before continuing.

"Oh," was all I could muster in response. What do you say to something like that?

"He was hitting her and she stopped fighting back. I got scared, so I jumped on him to make him stop. Usually I just stay in my room until it's over," Colin replied without looking up. He said it like the fighting wasn't anything out of the ordinary for him. He had stopped crying now, but an occasional hitch in his breathing would make his whole body convulse as he spoke.

"How did he give you those bruises?" I

knew I was taking a chance, yet I had to ask.

"I left a bike chain I was going to fix on the kitchen table. He grabbed it and sat on me. He just kept smacking me with it over and over. I told him to stop, but...."

Colin's voice trailed off. I wasn't sure how you could get bruises like that on both sides of your legs from the way he described what happened. I was about to ask him, then it occurred to me that he must have flipped him over and continued on the other side. I wanted to throw up as the image entered my mind. This guy was really twisted.

"Did you tell someone?" I asked.

"My mom tells me I can't. Says she will fix it. Said that 'bout a thousand times. I hate him so much. You can't tell anyone," Colin said as he looked down at his shaking hands.

"Okay," I replied, and I wasn't going to tell anyone. I am not sure why I said what I said next. I just felt like I owed him something now. Or maybe I really did want to talk about it. If that was the case, I certainly could have thought of a more sympathetic audience to open up to. "My dad's gone because he hit me, too. Down in Jackson. He'll be locked up for ten more years." I pulled up the right side of my shirt and showed him seven round scars that run down the side of my body in a jagged formation from my armpit to my waist. I don't remember when I got them because I was only three years old, but I do know that there are exactly seven. I know this because I count them with my fingers as I lay in bed at night, every night. Call it my own personal lullaby. Some kids get "Twinkle, Twinkle Little Star" — I get a constant reminder of how much my own dad didn't love me.

I told you at the beginning of this story that I ate because I hated myself. That's not entirely true. I also eat because I hate my father. Why self-medicate with food, you ask? I guess because it's easier to get than drugs, and it's not illegal. Not that I'd ever try those things. Like I said before, I'm fat, not stupid.

I only have one memory of dear old Dad. It's more about him than of him, though. I remember coloring at the kitchen table when my mom burst into the room frantically and scooped me up. I was terrified because she was obviously upset. When you are three, and the person that you believe is the strongest woman in the world is that scared, it is hard to comprehend what is happening. She carried me to the back bedroom, slammed the door, and we hid under the bed. She told me that we had to be very still and quiet, or the "bad guys" were going to get us. Her voice sounded different than I had ever heard it before. It was more panicky somehow. I remember her right eye was bleeding, because when she pulled me close to her under the bed some of the blood got in my hair. Her breath was rancid, and I could feel her fingernails cutting into my shoulder as she squeezed me.

Seconds later the door splintered open with the loudest noise I'd ever heard. Mom put her hand over my mouth to stifle my scream. I could feel the vibrations in my chest from my dad's boots as he stomped around the bedroom, angrily calling my mom's name. We hid there until we heard a commotion coming from the front yard. Dad ran out of the room, screaming at what turned out to be the cops. We heard gunshots and more screaming. I didn't really know what was going on because I was so little, but I do remember hoping that it was my dad that had gotten shot. I was instantly ashamed of myself for thinking that way. I am not ashamed of it anymore. My mom and I held each other, crying, until a policeman poked his head under the bed and told us to come out, it was safe now.

I was way too young to understand what was going on at the time. A few years later, when I was about nine, Mom tried to explain it all to me. I had already figured out that he was in prison and wasn't coming back anytime soon, but apparently she wanted to make sure I knew why. She said that he was locked up for hurting her, hurting me, and for pulling a gun on the police officers that shot him in our front yard. I'd kind of already figured all of this out, but it gave me an odd sense of comfort knowing for sure that he wasn't going to come busting through the door again in the near future.

Sometimes I lay awake at night and try to imagine what it would be like if he was dead. They did shoot him—only in the leg, though. Twice. He was arrested, and has been locked up ever since. That was my last memory of my dad. I can barely even tell you what his face looks like.

I can't remember, and there aren't any pictures of him anywhere in our house. My mom never went to visit him, and I certainly wasn't going to bring it up.

"Whoa! That must have hurt. Did he stab you?" Colin asked as he gaped at the wounds running down by side.

"Not sure if it hurt. I was too little to remember them. They are from cigarettes. My mom told me that he did it when he was drunk one night and I wouldn't stop crying." But that isn't entirely true either. She didn't tell me that until I was in third grade. Up until then she told me they were "Angel Marks." She said only really special little kids got them when the angels held on to them tighter because they didn't want to let them go down to Earth. That story used to make me feel special. Ironic, huh? I could feel my tears welling up again, but I fought them back this time.

"That sucks. Sorry," Colin said as he continued to stare down at his hands.

"Not your fault my dad was an ass," I replied.

"No. I'm just sorry," Colin mumbled.

"Sorry for what?" I asked.

"Everything."

I wasn't sure how to respond. I did feel bad for him because of what his dad did to him, but my dad was a prick too, and I didn't treat people like he did. Part of me wanted to give him a hug and part of me wanted to slam his balls in a locker. I had a choice to make. I could use what I now knew about Colin to get even in some way—hurt his feelings, tell people about how he cried, or even blackmail him. Or I could do what I always wished somebody would have done for me; make things better. I looked over and saw two tear tracks streaming down his cheeks and dripping off the end of his bulldog-like nose. No matter how much I hated him, no one should be that sad.

I didn't want to go on avoiding kids like Colin my whole life, but I didn't want to try and become Max the Bully Slayer, either. I just wanted all this pain to go away. Desperately. Maybe if we could just agree that our lives sucked and keep it our little secret, things would get better. I really don't think those other kids would pick on me as much if Colin wasn't leading the charge.

Finally I nodded and said, "It's okay. Worse things have happened to me. Obviously."

"Please don't tell anyone, Max," Colin whispered through the snot, sniffles, and tears that seemed to have taken over his face.

"I won't. You promise, too?" I asked without looking at him.

"Promise. And Max, I really am sorry."

I could tell that he really was kind of sorry. As mean he can be, I don't think he could have faked what I was seeing. I was curious as to why he was telling me (of all people) this. "Colin, why did you tell me about your dad? You were a complete jerk to me just this morning," I said.

"Why'd you tell me about your dad?" Colin shot back.

"I asked first," I replied.

He stared at the lockers across from us and thought on it for a second or two. "Dunno. Nobody ever asked me before, and I don't have anybody else to tell, I guess. Looks like we both got a problem with our dads. Sucks."

"Sure does," I said after glancing up at the clock, "Gym is almost over. We better get moving," I added as I stood and wiped my own face. This was more than enough "together time" for me with Colin. Besides, who knows how the other kids would react if they saw this hot mess when they came in through the locker room doors.

Colin stood too and walked back towards his locker. As he was beginning to pull his regular clothes back out, Mr. Drummond came bursting through the door.

"Where have you two been?" he asked, looking obviously confused. "Colin, I told you, one more unexcused absence and you were done. Your butt and a chair in the detention room are about to get to know each other real well." I told you, bullies always have clever jokes, and Mr. Drummond was definitely a bully. Colin just stared at him as he continued his little grandstanding tirade. "I am going to call your folks right now," Mr. Drummond told him, pointing a chubby finger at his chest.

"You can't do that!" Colin screamed. It sounded like anger, but I could hear the terror in his voice. To be honest, I was scared for him. Who knows what his father might do to him next time?

"Why not?" growled Mr. Drummond.

"Because he was helping me," I interrupted. What was I doing? It's amazing how quickly feelings change. One class period ago I had wanted to see Colin burned at the stake—forty-five minutes later I was putting my own neck on the line to help him out. Maybe it had something to do with all those hormones people are always saying middle schoolers have.

"Helping you with what?" snapped Mr. D.

"I fell in my last class and was having a hard time walking. Colin helped me get my stuff and come to class. Sorry we are so late. Totally my fault, Mr. Drummond," I finished without taking a breath. I reached into my pocket, pulled out the pass from Mr. Davis, faked a limp as I made my way across the locker room, and handed it to him.

Mr. Drummond looked over the pass and shot us both a suspicious look, but decided there was enough meat on my story to make it believable. "Okay. Don't let it happen again, or you guys will be with me on the track at 6 a.m. Got it?"

"Yes, sir," I replied. Mr. Drummond twirled around in his sausage casing/running suit and headed to his office.

Colin was staring back down at his hands, trying to not let them shake. He dressed quickly as his cronies came pouring back into the locker room to get dressed. He didn't say anything to me. He did look at me and give an almost unnoticeable nod. I knew that he wasn't going to carry me out of the locker room on his shoulders, professing our new friendship to the world, but I did expect a little more than what I got next.

"Dude, we were afraid Max-a-Million-Tons here had eaten you or something!"

"Yeah, they only gave him two trays at lunch today!"

Colin's buddies were doing what they always did; laying into me because they knew I wasn't going to fight back. After all I had been through today, I'd had enough. I was opening my mouth to say something, anything, back to them when Colin beat me to the punch.

Now, this still wasn't the noble Bully-and-Tormentor-Skip-Off-Into-the-Sunset- Together moment that most people would expect, but it was better than nothing.

"Dumbass, we haven't had lunch yet," Colin said without looking at me.

"Oh, well, I bet he's still really hun—"

"Shut up. You sound like an idiot. Let's get the hell out of here. I get to sit next to Hilary Grant next hour in math," Colin said as his stooges high-fived him and made lewd comments about things with girls that they really knew nothing about.

The idiot parade marched past me, making sure to give me a shoulder or two as they did. Colin looked up quickly and made eye contact, but nothing more. Colin may not have come galloping to my rescue, but he didn't join in, and in his own way he had told them to knock it off. It wasn't a total victory, but like I said before, I take what I can get.

CHAPTER 9

Once everyone else had left the locker room I got myself dressed and headed back toward my locker to get my books for Spanish class. I had been in the class for several weeks, and the only thing I knew how to say was, *¿Me permite ir al baño, por favor?* Translation: May I use the restroom, please? The only reason I learned that much was because our teacher, Ms. Castillo, never said no if you asked correctly. I would ask every other day, and sit in a stall for fifteen minutes or so before heading to class. Pathetic, I know, but still better than dodging spitballs and insults all hour.

I was contemplating whether I wanted to use my "bathroom pass" today or not when I walked past Michael Dryden digging furiously through his locker. I usually tried to avoid Michael because of my Two-Targets-is-Easier-Than-One philosophy, and because I enjoyed breathing through my nose. However, there was no one in the hall and I was feeling pretty good about what had just happened with Colin, so I thought I would spread a little joy.

"Hey, Mike. How's it going?" I said as I walked towards him.

I had never seen anyone turn around as quickly as Michael did at that moment. His speed was alarming, but it was the look in his eyes that really caught me off guard. He looked as furious as I had ever seen anyone in my life. His eyes were red, as if he had been crying, and he was breathing very heavily. Maybe that wasn't pink eye I thought I saw that morning on the bus. He quickly stuffed a balled-up sweatshirt into the bottom of his locker. I was too distracted by those eyes to pay much attention to anything else though.

Michael glared at me as I walked by, but didn't say a word. I repeated myself, and he finally responded with a grunt and a shrug of his shoulders. I could tell something was wrong, and usually I would have attempted to make a quick escape, but like I said before, things just felt different today.

I stopped and turned back toward him. "You okay?" Duh. Of course he wasn't okay.

"Stupid jerks," Michael mumbled as he turned back towards his closed locker. He fumbled with the lock for a second or two before blurting, "Do you ever just get sick of it?" His face was red and animated.

"What happened?" I had a pretty good idea. Us targets can spot each other from a mile away.

"They just never stop!" He snapped as he slammed his two closed fists into his thighs. He was beginning to look as if he might break into a crying fit, but pulled himself back together with a noticeable effort and a deep breath. Thank god. I didn't know if I could have handled another emotional breakdown that day.

"Who are you talking about?" I asked.

"Colin!" Michael grunted. "He and that jerk Anthony called my house last night. My little sister, Kathy, answered the phone."

I wasn't surprised at all to hear Colin's

name. He wasn't the only kid that picked on Michael, but he was definitely the most ruthless. Michael was as dirty and poor as I am fat, and Colin reminded him of it every chance he got. Michael lived in the old trailer park out on River Road. The only time most people ever see or even think about it is when there is a news story about a drug bust, an abused child, or worse happening there.

I had been to Michael's house once, for a birthday party in third grade. I remember the whole house smelling like cat piss and cigarette smoke. There was one couch in the middle of the living room. It was the kind of place that you could tell your parents were nervous about leaving you, but not enough to give up a few hours of freedom. On both sides, pizza boxes were stacked up waist high. All ten or so of us at the party sat on or near the couch and waited for the festivities to begin. His mom had made a small cake, and she put on cartoons for us to watch after we sang "Happy Birthday" to him. It was obvious that she was doing her best to make the day special, but the whole time we were there we could hear his older brother and his girlfriend fighting loudly in the next room. If *Saturday Night Live* was to create a skit making fun of trailer parks, it would have looked exactly like that party. It wasn't pretty. I did remember his sister, Kathy, because she sat on his lap and helped him blow out his candles. She was three or four at the time, and obviously adored him. I couldn't help but think about how happy they looked together that day, despite the crappy situation they were in.

Now, as we stood there in the hall, Michael's voice was getting higher and less stable with each word. I could tell that he was close to losing it. His hands were shaking and his forehead was all scrunched up like he was going to cry. I debated telling him about Colin's dad, but decided against it. I wasn't ready to let that cat out of the bag. Besides, I didn't think he'd be too sympathetic at the moment.

"They asked her if her big brother was taking a shower. When she said no, they told her I should be. Then they hung up, laughing," Michael said as tears welled up in his eyes.

"That's not so bad. Screw those idiots," I tried to reassure him.

"This morning she made a joke about it," he practically sobbed. "'Shouldn't you be in the shower?'" Michael said, imitating his sister's sing-song voice. I could feel the anger building in him. "I don't care what Colin thinks, but my little sister? She actually thinks I am worth something. You should have seen the look in her eyes when she hung up. She's eight years old, Max. Eight. She shouldn't look at her big brother that way. She's the closest thing to a friend I've got. She was laughing at me. Laughing! I want to kill them!"

Whoa. He was more upset than I thought, and it was a good thing we were alone. Principals and teachers don't take threats like that lightly.

I have never been a big brother, but I could kind of understand what he was saying. This was a kid that had thought he was the coolest thing in the world, and now she didn't. It would be nice to have a "built in" friend like that, and I could completely understand how lonely he would have felt without her. To be honest, it made me think that feeling sorry for myself because I got called names seem pretty stupid.

"That sucks, man. She will forget about it.

Don't worry," I told him very unconvincingly.

"I know. It's almost over now," Michael responded. He seemed to be looking through me, rather than at me. Creepy.

Just then Mrs. Montoya, our principal, came out of her office. "Everything okay here?"

"Do I look okay?" Michael snarled at her. Wow. This kid had balls.

"Excuse us, Marty. Mr. Dryden and I are going to need a minute alone," Mrs. Montoya said calmly. She got my name wrong. Shocker.

They walked past me and through the double doors of the main office. Before she closed the shades on her office window, I saw her pick up the phone and begin to dial. Michael sat pouting in the chair in front of her desk. I guessed that she was probably calling someone at home to come get him. If I was him, I would have been happy about that. I certainly wish I could have gone home early that day.

Chapter 10

Once Mrs. Montoya closed the blinds on her office windows I continued on to Spanish class. I was late, of course, but luckily Ms. Castillo was in a good mood today.

"*Hola, Senor Hefler. Como esta*?" asked Ms. Castillo. Translation: Hello, Mr. Hefler. How are you?

My response, "*Um, rojo*?" Translation: Um, Red?

Smooth.

I hate Spanish. However, I do love my Spanish teacher. Not only is Ms. Castillo an absolute sweetheart, she looks like she just fell out of one of those swimsuit catalogues that come in the mail. Besides the curves, she also had long, curly, dark brown hair, and the most amazing deep brown eyes. She was also very tall compared to the girls my age, and she always had the faintest smell of coconut and suntan lotion. As if all of this wasn't enough, she liked to wear little sundresses that would show off her legs. What's a teenage boy to do? If Mexico ever makes a travel brochure, she should be on the cover. I don't know what else they do down there, but they certainly got her right.

Anyways, she was a knock out, and every time she spoke Spanish in that little R-rolling accent of hers I could feel my heart melting (amongst other sensations....). I would sit in class and listen to her all day and watch her walk back and forth across the room—if they would let me. But even with all of that going for her, I think the reason I was really so attracted to her was the fact that she never looked at me without smiling. Honestly, she is the only person in my life I can say that about.

"Haha! Oh, Maxwell. You are so funny," Ms. Castillo giggled as she put her left hand on my chest and swung her right arm across my shoulders. She then began to walk me toward my desk. "Who did you get that marvelous sense of humor from?"

Across. My. Shoulders. I wasn't just speechless, I was breathless. This was about as much female contact as I'd had in my life up to that point. I went from not knowing Spanish to forgetting English, too. All I could manage was, "*Si.*"

Ms. C let that cute little giggle slip out again as she gave me a one-armed squeeze and dropped me off in the front row. Best seat in the house.

As I sat there drooling on my desk, I couldn't help but think about how my morning had gone. Did I really just have a meaningful conversation with Colin Culler, or as close as you can get to one with him? Did I really tell him about my dad? I don't think I had ever mentioned that to anyone but my mother, and a few counsellors that I was forced to see after he went away. The scary part was that now Colin had a piece of me. He knew something that he could use against me if he really wanted to hurt me. But I had a piece of him, too. A bigger piece. Everyone already thought I was a loser — he had a reputation to protect. I don't think I even have it in me to do something like that to someone else, but I guess I would if I had to. I really didn't think Colin would take a chance on finding out.

And then there was Michael. I really didn't like him a whole lot, but we definitely had quite a bit in common. We should be sticking together, but there was something about him that I just didn't trust. Don't get me wrong. I am sure that there are a thousand reasons to not like me, too. But I consider myself to be pretty stable. I didn't get that feeling from Michael. He made me nervous. It was like he was always on the verge of a meltdown. Maybe his skin just wasn't as thick as mine — no pun intended.

Chapter 11

Once I was done contemplating, and drooling, I used my mastery of the Spanish language to ask permission to use the restroom. Ms. Castillo, with that sweet, sweet smile of hers, wrote me a pass and I was off for my daily break.

I turned the corner by the water fountain and grabbed a quick drink before heading for the little boys' room. Just as I was about to push the door open, someone caught my eye from down the hall.

It was Michael again. He was exiting the front doors of the school and walking very quickly, almost running, towards the parking lot. I guessed they sent him home and he was being picked up outside. Across the hall, Mrs.

Montoya was standing in the office door with her arms folded across her chest and a very concerned look on her face. Apparently Michael had given her enough trouble for one day. He was out of there—lucky bastard.

When he was out of sight, I entered the restroom for a little "me time." I didn't stay as long as usual. Maybe it was because of all I had been through that morning; maybe it was because I hadn't gotten enough of Ms. C for the day. But for some reason being alone wasn't where I wanted to be for once.

I walked back into Spanish class and was greeted once again by that brilliant smile as I headed towards my seat. I was a bit surprised, but not totally shocked, to find Jackson Torres sitting where I had left my stuff before leaving the room. My books had been moved back three seats down the row. I shot him a dirty look as I turned sideways and shimmied down the aisle to my books. I knew what he was up to—a better view. He just smiled at me and moved his eyebrows up and down like the actors in the old movies my mom watches do whenever they get done saying something clever. I was annoyed, but not mad. I would have done the same thing if I were him. The smell of coconut and sun screen was a lot stronger in the front row.

CHAPTER 12

"*Adios!*" hollered Mrs. C from her desk as the bell rang dismissing us from third hour. Time for math class. I really don't mind math. I know a lot of kids hate it, and I think most adults, too. But for me there is something comforting about absolute, black and white, right or wrong answers. It's not like English class, where an answer can be kind of right, but not completely. Or like P.E., where my size holds me back no matter what is going on in my head. No, in math class you know where you stand on every question. Right or wrong. No wiggle room. No maybes or ifs. I don't have many situations in my life that are that well defined.

As I made my way down the hall I couldn't help but notice again that today just felt different. I didn't automatically look at the ground when making eye contact with people. I didn't get a queasy feeling in my stomach every time someone said my name. I even felt lighter somehow. I don't know, it was just a different kind of day. Based on the way it had started — the bus ride — I didn't expect much to come of the next seven hours. But as I walked down the hall with my head up instead of studying my shoes, I noticed a few things. When you are as big as I am, and have been through the torment I've experienced, you start to just assume some things. For example, I just assumed that when I was in public most people were scowling at me with a look of disgust on their faces. Or that people intentionally went out of their way to avoid seeing or talking to me. I had become so conditioned to avoid human contact because of these assumptions that it had been forever since I had even bothered to try. But today — today was different. I looked up as I walked down the hall. People weren't looking at me with disgust; most people weren't really looking at me at all. But a couple of the ones that were even managed to smile or nod in my direction.

It was kind of like a movie I saw once. There was this guy that was stranded on what he thought was a deserted island. He lived there for years in a cave, scared to go out further than he had to and explore his surroundings. Eventually he had enough of the cave and ventured out. He climbed to the top of a cliff and looked over the peak to the other side. Turns out there was an entire city down there the whole time. When I first saw it I thought, *What a chump. This loser wasted half of his life because he was scared of a couple of monkeys or bananas or something*. As I walked down the halls of Lincoln Middle School that day, it dawned on me — I was no different. It was time to not be scared anymore and get out of my cave. I wasn't about to sign up for the school play or run for class president just yet, but I knew I was done hiding. I didn't know what was on the other side of that cliff, but I knew it had to be better than where I had been.

I strolled confidently into Mrs. Jacobs' math class and gave her a smile and a wave. I must have caught her off guard, because she stopped what she was doing at the whiteboard and looked around as if she wasn't sure I was talking to her. "Hi, M-Max. How are you today?" she asked.

"Doin' great, Mrs. J. Are we doing fractions today?"

"Sure are, Max. I don't think I've ever seen a student smile while using that word before," she commented with a sarcastic little smile of her own.

Mrs. Jacobs is probably in her late thirties, but could easily pass for a student teacher. She looked much younger than her years, and acted it, too. My favorite part about Mrs. Jacobs is her laugh. She has one of those overpowering, cackling, from the bottom of her soul type of laughs. You can't hear it and not smile, no matter what else was going on in your world at that moment. As shy as I am around most people, I always have an urge to joke around and try to make her release that contagious laugh. It's like sunshine for my ears. The woman just oozes pure joy.

Her class was probably about as much fun as a math class could be. Most kids like math just a little less than driving a hot nail through their own eyeball. Those of us lucky enough to have Mrs. Jacobs for math didn't have that problem. It was still math, but it was bearable.

I smiled back at her and strutted—yes, I said strutted—toward my usual seat in the last row near the bulletin board. I slid sideways to the second to last seat and started to sit down.

That's when my "feel-good" bubble burst. As I moved my ample backside towards the ugly blue chair that drew the unlucky job of supporting me day after day, I started to notice something out of the ordinary. Either my chair was smaller, or I was losing weight, because I had already sunk past where I would normally make contact, and had yet to feel that hard plastic push back against me. Then it hit me—I had no chair. I had a split second to make this realization, and even less time to do something about it.

Too late. I tumbled to the floor, dropping my books on the way down in a clumsy attempt to catch my balance, and rolled backwards, hitting my head on the desk behind me. There was one second of shocked silence before the class erupted into laughter. I struggled to get back to a seated position and try to look halfway casual about the whole thing. It didn't work. As I scrambled to sit up, I put my right hand on the empty seat next to me and my left hand on my math book and started to push myself up. Unfortunately, neither of these immovable objects was able to withstand my unstoppable bulk and both slid out to my sides, leaving me to crash down to the floor yet again.

The laughter continued and intensified. Mrs. Jacobs ran over and started to help me up. She gripped my upper arm and tried to help me to my feet, but my skin was so slippery with perspiration that I crashed down to the floor for a third time. By this point the laughter that was focused solely on me had now dissipated into distracted chatter. Apparently even when I am being humiliated I am not interesting enough to keep people's attention. I think that pissed me off as much as the fall did.

I was finally able to get up by rolling to the side, getting my knees up under me, and using the wall to pull myself up.

"You okay, Max?" asked Mrs. Jacobs. "Let me grab you a chair."

I angrily swung my head from side to side,

looking for who had moved my chair in the first place. I was sure someone had pulled it out from under me. That's when I saw it. My chair was next to the door, with a hand written sign taped to it that said, "Broken, please replace." I just didn't look before I sat. Completely my fault, but it didn't make it any less embarrassing or infuriating.

I could feel the anger building inside of me. I have been embarrassed plenty of times in my life—I know how to handle that. But this was different. I have been so sad that I haven't been able to stop crying (See Bus Incident). But I had never been so mad that I couldn't control myself. It was like watching a shaken two liter of pop start to fizz up when the top was opened, only this time I couldn't put the top back on fast enough.

"No! Stop it!" I screamed at Mrs. Jacobs as I waved her away from me. It felt like I was watching myself in a movie. I shoved my desk to the side, threw my notebook on the floor, and turned to face my classmates.

"Max! Calm down!" pleaded Mrs. Jacobs.

But I couldn't. My chest felt like it was being

squeezed by a belt, and I could feel my heart beating in my temples. Usually at a moment like this I want to just disappear. Not this time. I am not sure when it exactly happened—maybe when Colin confided in me, maybe when Mr. Davis stuck up for me in English class, maybe when Mrs. Castillo put her arm around me like I wasn't repulsive—but something had "clicked" inside of me. I didn't want to disappear this time. That feeling of embarrassment was replaced with a burning desire to physically hurt everyone that was looking at me and laughing at that moment.

"You calm down! Don't tell me what to do! All of you shut up!" The looks on my classmates' faces were ones that I didn't recognize at first. It was the way you look at a dog that you just realized isn't playing anymore and really wants to bite you. I felt more powerful and free than I ever had when I saw those faces looking back at me. I also felt extremely frustrated and helpless. I knew I wasn't really going to attack my whole math class, but THEY didn't know that. Now I knew what the bully felt like. Fear. Equals. Control. I had just gotten a taste of the dark side, and I am ashamed to say that I liked it.

"Max! I am going to have to ask you to leave the room until you can control yourself," Mrs. Jacobs said as firmly and calmly as she could manage. They must train teachers on how to pick just the right tone for situations like this. Despite all my rage, that "teacher voice" and look sunk in.

I angrily stomped towards the door. Just as I was turning the corner at the top of my row and making a right towards the exit, Anthony, one of Colin's stooges, leaned closer to me, put his hand on my shoulder, and loudly hollered out, "Don't worry, Max. Maybe they'll give you an extra cupcake or ten today at lunch to make you feel better." As he said this he stuck out his bottom lip like he was pouting, and pretended to rub tears from his eye with his other hand.

Anthony was one of my least favorite people at Lincoln. He usually wasn't smart or brave enough to pick on anyone on his own. He typically just acted like Collin's little parrot and repeated his insults like an echo. Even a bully deserves some credit for originality. Anthony had a big fat zero on the scoreboard in that category.

Now, I had heard people say that you should "think before you act" a billion times, but I always thought it was a dumb saying, because of course your brain has to have a thought before you can act on it. In a split second I learned that that saying did have a purpose. Without even realizing that they were my arms, I instinctively shot both hands out into Anthony's chest. I am not a very strong kid, but 230 pounds is going to move anybody that is unlucky enough to be in the way. Anthony's head snapped back and he started to stumble back towards the desks behind him. He landed in one of these desks and his momentum took him completely over it, crashing head first into the ground.

"Don't ever touch me again!"

I didn't stick around to wait for Anthony's reaction. I continued into the hall, slammed the door behind me, and headed straight for Principal Montoya's office.

CHAPTER 13

I was now in uncharted territory. Not only had I never really stood up for myself before, I had also never really been in trouble. When you work as hard as I do to fade into the background, you tend to not be noticed for any reason, good or bad. I knew that now I was going to be on the radar. Word would spread, and by the end of the day every adult in the building would have an eye on me at all times. I was sure the kids would too. At first it would be because they were a little scared of me. But eventually all this attention would just make the target on my ass a lot brighter. Like a billboard. A big neon billboard.

I was still pretty worked up as I rounded the corner by the boy's restroom and made my way towards the office. I was so completely distracted with thoughts of what I could possibly say to Mrs. Montoya to get out of this that I didn't even notice Mr. Mark mopping in the doorway.

"It's 'bout time," he said to himself without looking up.

I stopped dead in my tracks and looked back at him. "About time for what?" I sneered.

"'Bout time you had enough. I's was begin'n to think you'se wasn't ever goin' to get mad. Mad a good thing sometimes. It let everyone know you ain't goin to just take it all the time," Mr. Mark said without looking up from his mop.

He must have heard the whole thing. Mrs. Jacobs' room was very near the boys' restroom. I can't imagine some of the things that custodians must see and hear in a school. I didn't know what to say to him. I just stood and stared back at him with tears welling up in my eyes.

"You did good. I know a few other kids that I wish could have heard that. Would have done them 'lotta good. It do get better, Max, but not until they know you'se had enough. They knows now."

Mr. Mark continued to mop the floor outside of the boys' bathroom as I stood there contemplating those words. The realistic side of me thought that was a bunch of crap, and all I had done was throw a tantrum in front of twenty-five classmates and a pretty cool math teacher. The hopeful side of me thought that maybe he was right. Maybe now they did know that I'd had enough.

As I was standing there trying to make sense of all of this, Mr. Mark's walkie-talkie squawked. "If anyone sees Max Hefler in the building, please call the main office. Wearing black sweatpants and a navy blue hoodie."

"That sounds like you, big boy. Come on. I'll walk you down," Mr. Mark said as he put his mop back into his bucket and placed a SLIPPERY WHEN WET sign in front of the restroom door.

We walked down the hall, him looking straight ahead, me studying my shoes again.

"Mr. Mark?"

"Yeah?"

"Why does everyone hate me so much?" I

don't know why I was asking him this. I can't say what I expected to hear him say to a question like that, but his answer caught me completely off guard.

Mr. Mark stopped abruptly and poked me right in the chest with one chubby index finger. "They don't hate you. You hates you, and they think you'se stupid and weak for it. They ain't hatin' you. They's feelin' sorry for you, Max. That be worse, if you ask me. You don't want all that pity. The ones that are pick'n on you just knows that you ain't gonna fight back, and it keeps the target off of them for a little while. Once they see that you like yourself, they will like you, too. I guarantee it," Mr. Mark very plainly stated without breaking eye contact with me as he put his hand on my back. I could tell that he meant it, because his eyes were starting to mist up, too.

It was great advice, but easier said than done. We walked in silence the rest of the way to the office. He opened the door to let me in. His massive hand seemed to swallow the whole doorknob as he turned it. I actually felt a little small next to Mr. Mark.

I entered and took two steps towards Principal Montoya's office before stopping to turn back towards Mr. Mark, but he had already closed the door and left. I never did get the chance to thank him.

CHAPTER 14

"Max Hefler," called the secretary. "Mrs. Montoya will see you now."

I had calmed down considerably by this point. I wasn't sure what had gotten into me in Mrs. Jacobs' room, but it had passed. All that rage drained out of me as quickly as it had filled me up. Sometimes the ups and downs of being fourteen make a roller coaster look like the merry-go-round. I wonder if all kids that "lose it" like I just did feel this way afterwards.

I stood up slowly from the row of chairs that sat across from the main office desk, and shuffled the thirty feet to the principal's office. I stopped for a second to study the glass door with Mrs. Montoya's name stenciled across it. I had always wondered what the other side of that door looked like. As I said, I had never been in real trouble before. I had also never been in that office for a good reason. Our school has Students of the Month and Citizenship Awards, and a ton of other stupid little honors that younger kids love. In middle school you are supposed to act annoyed or bored when you win something like that. I never had a chance to see how I felt about it because I never won. But to be honest, it would have been nice.

"Have a seat, um…." Mrs. Montoya looked down at the pink discipline form to check for my name. She obviously didn't know it, but I wasn't too offended. It just proves that my "Fat Kid Camo" was working. "Um, Max. Please sit, Max."

I plopped down into the hard, wooden chair and looked down at my hands. I wasn't sure if I should say something or wait for her to speak. I decided to play it safe.

"Well, do you have anything to say before I get started?" asked Mrs. Montoya.

"I'm sorry," I replied, and I was. Not for sticking up for myself or pushing Anthony. I was sorry for giving Mrs. Jacobs such a hard time.

"Well, sometimes 'Sorry' just isn't enough, Max." She stood up, obviously flustered—maybe from dealing with Michael earlier? —and pointed her finger directly in my face. "I will not allow you to bully one more child. Not on my watch!" she shouted.

I couldn't believe my ears. She was calling me the bully! This was so damn stupid that I was having a difficult time wrapping my brain around it. Was she freaking blind? Didn't she know that I was the most tormented kid in this crappy school? I was speechless.

"But, Mrs. Montoya—"

"Save it. Once you lay your hands on another student you are a bully. Period. End of discussion."

She had a point. Usually I was on the receiving end, but today I had dished it out, too. I really couldn't argue with her logic, but I couldn't help but wonder if she ever had this conversation with any of the kids that picked on me. I doubted it, because they were much more clever about how they went about it. I, unfortunately, chose the "Match in a Fireworks

Factory" approach.

"Now I get to call poor Anthony Herndon's mother and explain why her baby, her only child, has a head injury and is bawling in the nurse's office!" Mrs. Montoya bellowed.

Bawling, huh? I couldn't help myself. I made Anthony cry—I could barely contain my smile. I fought it back as hard as I could because I didn't think Mrs. Montoya would have reacted very well.

"I'm sorry," I replied—but I wasn't really. "I didn't mean to hurt anyone." I really didn't.

"Well, this is your first offense," Mrs. M said as she took a deep breath, straightened her skirt, and sat back down. "It's almost lunch time. There is no point in sending you back to Mrs. Jacobs' room today, but you do owe her and Anthony an apology. You will also be serving three days of after school detention. Mr. Mark could use some help. You'll be on cleaning duty. Of course, I will have to call your mother as well." Mrs. Montoya turned her attention back to the discipline form on her desk and scribbled her signature at the bottom.

"Yes, ma'am."

That could have been worse. I didn't have lunch detention, and I really didn't mind the idea of spending more time with Mr. Mark. I wasn't worried at all about my mom getting a call from the school. She would understand — heck, she might even be proud of me. She would put on the typical "I raised you better than that" speech that all parents are required to give in these situations, but no real punishment would come from it.

Mrs. M tore off the pink carbon-copy detention form, handed it to me, and asked me to take a seat back in the waiting area outside of her office until the bell that released us to lunch went off. I mumbled another apology and quickly made for the door. I took a seat on the same uncomfortable chair that I had sat in while waiting to learn my fate just a few minutes ago.

I should have been a little scared at that point. I'd pissed off Anthony, Mrs. Jacobs was probably very disappointed in me, and my mom was sure to get a phone call. Despite all of this, I was in a good place. Along with all that bad stuff, I had also had a few highlights today. I had a good talk with Colin and possibly got him off of my butt for a little while, Mr. Davis went out of his way to help me out, and I made Anthony cry. I. Made. Anthony. Cry. That one was my favorite. It's kind of ironic that the first day I ever got into real trouble was also the first day that I ever really felt good about myself.

CHAPTER 15

The bell rang signaling the start of my best subject, lunch. I know what you're thinking. Why would I say something like that about myself when I hear it from the Colins of the world all day? I say things like that because I have learned that it's better to laugh at myself before anyone else uses the opportunity to get laughs at my expense. A therapist that my mom made me see for a while called it my, "Comedy Shield." She said I was avoiding the "real issues." What she didn't get, and I didn't want to tell her because I knew it would upset my mom, was that I usually have two choices in most situations; make the jokers laugh or fight back. I learned at an early age that I was even less of a fighter than I was a lover. It only

100

took roughly a dozen butt-kickings to learn this valuable lesson.

I have heard more fat/lunch/feedbag/All-You-Can-Eat jokes than any other kid on Earth. To be perfectly honest, I find some of them funny, too. The only times they really hurt is when they have a little bit of truth to them. I do eat a lot—no denying that—but the worst part about it is that I know what I am doing to myself, but I just can't seem to stop. Sometimes it's about the taste, but most of the time it's just because shoveling things that taste good into my mouth makes me feel better for a few moments. Unfortunately, that good feeling is immediately replaced by regret. Every. Time.

My mom tried to get me to exercise by signing me up for baseball, taking me to the park, going for walks with me, stuff like that. But none of it ever stuck. We quit baseball because we didn't have a car to get me to practice. The park got boring. She became too busy to go for walks. All the typical excuses. She even tried buying me a Wii last year. What a joke. I now have very fit forearms, and the only use it gets is as a place to set my Mountain Dew while I play Xbox. At this point I think she has kind of given up on the idea of exercise. For a while she tried to get us to eat healthier stuff like fruits and vegetables. It was horrible. Eventually that stopped too, because she didn't have the time or money to make meals like that all the time.

My worst eating binges always seem to happen when things are rough between my mom and me. She's really the closest thing I have to a friend — my mom's my best friend. I know. I would make fun of me for that, too. Even when school sucks I know I can come home and count on her to cheer me up. She really is a wonderful person. No matter what else she has going on in her life, she always makes me feel like the main attraction when we are together.

As I get older and think back to things that happened when I was a little kid, I can kinda see that she really had no idea how to raise a child. I never really had a bedtime, and most of our meals came from a drive-thru window. We were always broke, even though it felt like she worked a million jobs. Sometimes she left me with some questionable babysitters, like the lady that sent me to the 7-11 on the corner for smokes when I was eight. She was a real treat. Or the guy that thought that lighting off firecrackers in the backyard was an acceptable activity for a nine-year-old. Needless to say, a first-class day care just wasn't in the budget.

It's easy to forget that she got into this whole "family thing" thinking she was going to have a partner to help her through it. My dad kind of left us both in a bad spot, but especially her. I wish I was half as strong as my mom.

So as you can imagine, when things are not good with Mom I really don't have anyone else to turn to, so I eat. And eat. And eat. Sometimes I get myself all hyped up on the idea that I am going to start fresh the next morning. I am going to eat healthy food and go for a walk instead of playing video games. Soon my life will look like one of those body spray commercials, where some scrawny dude has to fight off the chicks because they can't get enough of him.

Then life happens. Sometimes it's an event like what happened on the bus that morning, or Mom, thinking she's being nice, brings home a pizza, or something tastes good and I just can't stop. No matter what the cause is, the result is always the same. I feel bad. I eat until I feel good, then feel bad again because I ate so much. It's like the merry-go-round that never stops.

Luckily (or unfortunately) for me, the smell of nachos quickly and silently replaced these thoughts. I love nachos. I know, you're shocked, but I mean it. I. Literally. Love. Nachos. If you put Mrs. Castillo and nachos in the same room, I am not sure which one I would choose. Especially the school nachos. They are that good.

I waddled slowly over to the line and patiently waited my turn. I heard a couple of kids behind me whisper my name and giggle. I knew what they were doing, but nothing was going to get to me this afternoon. I was a new man. I turned to them and said, "Sorry guys. You're a little late. Everyone knows that if you are behind me in the lunch line, you are probably not eating today. I heard the salads are good." The two boys looked at each other, exchanged a confused look, and decided to search out their next victim in another line. Apparently my "Comedy Shield" was working just fine.

I smiled to myself as I turned back around. Time to eat my nachos. I'd worry about the weight tomorrow, and enjoy a little quiet time before heading off to science class. I might even try to sit next to someone new today.

I smiled at the lunch lady and thanked her—I am a rock star to the lunch ladies—before grabbing a handful of napkins and surveying the cafeteria for a seat. I decided that I wasn't feeling quite as brave as I thought, and dismissed the idea of making a new friend today. Instead, I spotted a seat over in the corner. On one side of me was the wall, on another side were the kids that spoke primarily Spanish—no worries about having to talk to anyone there—and a couple of rows back was Colin and his crew. I was just about to set my tray down when I felt two hands shove me square in the back. I fell into the lunch table and went belly first into my nachos. I stood back up and turned to face my attacker with cheese and chips plastered to the underside of my stomach.

It was Anthony. "You didn't really think I was just going to let you get away with that, did you?" He grabbed me by the front of my shirt and shoved me backwards. The back of my legs hit the bench of the cafeteria table and

I collapsed down on my butt. Before I could respond, he wound up and slapped me across the face as hard as he could. It sounded like a firecracker going off, and drew the attention of the entire cafeteria. The pain shot through my cheek and down my neck. I could feel the tears beginning to well up in my eyes. I choked them back as best as I could. There was no way I was giving Anthony the satisfaction of seeing me cry.

"I didn't want to push you. You didn't give me much of a choice. Mind your own business next time," I said in a voice slightly louder than a whisper. It is amazing how quickly confidence can be slapped out of a person.

Anthony was cocking back his other hand when Colin walked around my table and stood next to Anthony and me. "What's going on?" he asked Anthony.

Anthony dropped his hand and looked at Colin. "Tub-of-lard here got cute in math class and pushed me over a desk when I wasn't looking," replied Anthony as he raised his hand once again.

Colin reached up and grabbed his wrist.

"Dude, don't do this here. You want to get in trouble? We'll take care of this when we get off the bus," Colin reassured him.

"You're right. I'll see you after school, fat ass," Anthony whispered to me before he and Colin turned to walk away.

Colin shot me an almost nonexistent look before completely turning his back to me. I wasn't sure, but the look seemed to be saying, "Chill. I will take care of this."

They had barely taken two steps when a girl's high-pitched screech rose above the usual din of the cafeteria. Both Colin and Anthony stopped dead in their tracks. Everyone's head turned in the direction of the scream.

"Oh my god! Oh my god! He's got a gun!"

CHAPTER 16

The people on the other side of the commotion made a run for the cafeteria doors. Everyone on my side of Colin and Anthony sat frozen, because we could see the gun, and it was pointed in our direction. It was Michael Dryden, and all of his attention was focused on Colin Culler

I don't know what Michael was thinking. At first I thought that he must have been sent home and came back with his dad's gun or something. Then I remembered the balled up sweatshirt he had been stuffing in his locker earlier. It was pretty obvious that he was disturbed that morning, I just didn't have any idea how disturbed.

He stood with a wide stance and the gun

pointed directly at Colin. It was mostly black with a long barrel and dark wood on the handle. He had both hands wrapped so firmly around the grip of the pistol that his knuckles were white. It looked like he could barely hold it up. He didn't have a finger on the trigger, yet.

"You had no right! You can't talk to my sister like that! You ruined my life! Kathy thinks I'm a joke, and now you are going to pay for it!" Michael somehow screamed through clenched teeth. It took me a moment to realize it, but I think I was the only person in the room that had any idea what he was talking about. Earlier, in the hallway, he had told me about the prank call Colin and Anthony had made to his house. Something about how his sister looked at him now. It was so hard to remember all the details with a loaded gun just a few feet away.

Colin just stood there staring at the firearm pointed at his head. He was frozen. I imagine that I would be too in that situation. After the longest ten seconds of our lives he tried to open his mouth to defend himself.

"I don't—"

"Shut up! You've said enough. This is for

every kid that you've screwed with at this school." This last part he said in almost eerily calm voice, like he had made up his mind. Michael moved his finger from the handle of the gun to the trigger. Colin took a baby step backwards, but didn't dare run. He would have been an easy target. Anthony's mouth was wide open, and it looked like he had stopped breathing altogether.

"Michael. Please put the gun down. We are all here to help you." It was Principal Montoya. She must have slipped into the room when she heard the ruckus.

"The hell you are! I told you about him a thousand times! What did you do about it? Huh? Nothing!" Michael said without looking away from Colin for even a second. He began to walk closer.

He was right. Many people had reported Colin over the years, but he was always smooth enough to talk his way out of any serious trouble.

"Well, please, let me help you now. Come with me to my office and we can fix this, Michael," she pleaded.

"Too late. Shut your mouth or I will shoot everyone in this room," Michael declared. Mrs. Montoya stepped back and stopped talking.

My head was spinning. I knew why Michael felt the way he did, and I now knew why Colin did the things he'd done to all of us "targets" over the years. The kicker was that I was the only one in the room that knew BOTH of these things. I had to do something. I sat there for several more seconds, trying to decide if I wanted to continue to fade into the background or stand up and take my chances. Like I said before, there was something different about today. I stood up.

"Please, Michael. He's hurt me, too," I begged. I didn't dare move any closer because I didn't want to startle him. "But I don't want to see you spend the rest of your life in jail because of him, either."

"Oh, I won't."

A cold shiver ran down my back when he said those words. I think everyone in the room knew what he meant by that. He wasn't leaving alive either. Those words were a game changer.

"Please. Let's get out of here. You and me

can just go. Nobody else. Let's get the hell out of here, me and you." I didn't really want to run away, but I couldn't think of anything else to say.

"Too late, Max. I'm done." Michael moved another step closer to Colin. He was now about ten feet away. More than close enough to make sure he didn't miss.

I don't know how to explain what I did next, other than maybe pure panic. I stepped in front of Colin. Michael's glare broke and refocused on me. There was a glimpse of the old Michael in those eyes, but it was quickly pushed aside.

"What the hell? Are you on his side now? Don't do this, Max. I'm doing this for you, too. Get out of the way," he pleaded.

"I can't let you do this, Michael. He's hurt me too, but it doesn't have to be this way. This is stupid."

Just as those words left my mouth, Michael lunged forward, shoving the barrel of the gun directly into my mouth. The metal clicked violently against my top teeth and the sight scraped the roof of my mouth. My taste buds were overwhelmed by a mixture of saliva, blood, and gun oil. I stumbled back a step, but Michael kept the gun right where it was.

"It's not stupid! He's ruined my life. Now I'm going to take his. Don't make me take yours too!" He shouted at me. Michael was standing with both hands on the stock of the pistol, his feet spread wide, with the gun held at an angle that forced me to tilt my head slightly upward. I kept my hands out to my sides. I thought about trying to snatch the gun away, or at least out of my mouth, but then thought better of it. I was not quick enough for that kind of hero crap.

I could see in his eyes that he meant it. I can't say that I've ever been to that point, but I didn't doubt him for a second. I realized at that moment that there was no way that all of us were leaving the cafeteria alive that day. Someone was going to pay for Colin's sins, one way or another.

"Please don't make me shoot you, Max," Michael said in a mixture of a whisper and a cry. "Will you sit back down?" he pleaded. He was shaking violently. I slowly nodded, but I had no intention of sitting back down. Ninety nine out of a hundred times I would have jumped at that offer, but like I said, there was something different about today.

Michael jerked the barrel out of my mouth, once again scraping the sight along the roof of my mouth as he did so. My tongue was instantly coated with blood again. This should have been my chance to get the hell out of harm's way, but I didn't budge. Instead, I slowly turned and faced Colin.

"Colin, you are the biggest jerk that most of us have ever known." I wasn't exactly sure where I was going with this, but I felt like it needed to said, and I needed more time to think. "You have tormented me for two years, and countless other kids since they were little." I thought that maybe, if I could get some of the things I think Michael was feeling into words, he might decide that shooting isn't necessary.

Colin just stared at me in disbelief. This was a good thing. The last thing I wanted him to do was talk.

"If anyone of us had half the balls that Michael does, we would have shot you ourselves a long time ago."

I looked back over my shoulder at Michael.

Tears were quietly streaming down his cheeks now as he continued to point his pistol squarely at Colin. He was still obviously upset, but he wasn't demanding that I move anymore. I wasn't sure what to do next.

As my eyes shifted back to Colin, I noticed that most of the people in the cafeteria had slowly crept back towards the walls. Many had slipped out through the side doors. That wouldn't have been hard to do since all of Michael's focus had been on Colin since the whole thing started. So, at that moment in time, in the center of the cafeteria, was myself, Colin, Michael, Anthony, and a handful of other kids that were now too scared to move. I did notice that Principal Montoya had also moved back a couple more steps. What surprised me was that another adult, Mr. Mark, had now appeared in the picture.

"Don't worry, Max. I am going to take care of it for all of us," Michael hissed as he moved a step to his left to regain his line of sight with Colin. They were now no more than eight feet apart, with me right smack in the middle of them, and slightly to the right of Michael.

I was beginning to panic. I stood there in a cold sweat for what felt like minutes, but couldn't have possibly been that long, running through the possibilities in my mind. The way I saw it, any one of the following scenarios could play out at any moment:

Michael puts down the gun and we all go home. (My personal favorite, but not likely)

Michael shoots Colin and I can get to him before he shoots himself. (A plan that sounded a lot better two hours ago before my conversation with Colin)

I tackle Michael right now before anyone can get shot. (Once again, I am not much of a natural athlete.).

I decided that it had to be #3, and it had to be now. I slowly raised my hands and began to turn towards Michael. I didn't want to move too suddenly and scare him before I could make my move. I was mentally counting down from five, when a fourth scenario that never crossed my mind began to unfold.

CHAPTER 17

"You, stupid! Yeah, I talkin to you, skinny boy!" It was Mr. Mark. "You'se really gonna show him! He's gonna be sing'n with the angels, and you'se gonna be in Hell or jail fo' the rest of yo' life. Who's really losin' here?"

Michael was startled back into reality for a second. He looked over his shoulder to see who was talking to him without ever taking the gun off of Colin.

Mr. Mark approached the scene with that same rambling, stumbling walk we saw every day in the halls. He had a very intense look in eyes. No sign of a smile.

"Huh?" Michael grunted. "Stay away! I have no problem shooting you, too, fat man. What's one more?"

"You ain't shootin' nobody! You'se ain't got the stones, I don't care what chubby here says. He wouldn't be knowin' what stones be all about, anyways," Mr. Mark wheezed as he moved even closer to Michael.

"Shut up! I don't care about what some fat janitor thinks!" screamed Michael.

"You shore' do care what I's thinkin'. If you didn't, you woulda shot somebody by now."

"I said shut up!" Michael screamed again over his shoulder. "Don't tell me what to do!"

"You ain't gonna hurt nobody. Now put that damn gun down before I's have to come over there and put it down for you," Mr. Mark said as he continued his slow, ambling walk towards Michael.

He was starting to really piss Michael off. With a twisted look of pure anger on his face Michael whirled around, away from Colin, and pointed the gun directly at Mr. Mark.

The sound of the gunshot was deafening. It was like my ears had shut off. I stared at Michael as a look of absolute terror overtook his face. He dropped the gun and looked at his hands like they were foreign objects that he was noticing for the first time. The gun bounced off the cafeteria floor and skidded to a stop a few feet away from me. Once the initial shock wore off, I waddled over and kicked the gun under a nearby table so that Michael couldn't pick it up again and do anymore damage.

Kids were scattering in all directions. Colin suddenly came to his senses and bolted. He broke for the doors, knocking Anthony down along the way. Both of them sprinted to the furthest corner of the cafeteria and then out into the hallway.

Wait. Damage. A shot was fired. I spun around quickly and saw Mr. Mark's legs buckle. He dropped to his knees with his hands held together over his chest. He slowly pulled them away from his body and looked at them. I nearly passed out when I saw the amount of blood running between his fingers and down the front of his khaki uniform. Without looking up again, he fell forward onto his considerable stomach. Blood quickly pooled around his body.

At about this time my hearing returned. Kids were screaming as they sprinted towards the exit. To my left was Michael, still standing there in complete shock, watching Mr. Mark die. To my right was Principal Montoya. She was attending to Mr. Mark, trying to turn him over so that she could check his pulse or something. I knew he was dead as soon as Mrs. Montoya slipped and fell when her high heels slid through the bloody mess now surrounding his body. There was no way a person could lose that much blood and still be alive. It was soaking into her pretty pink pantsuit. Mr. Mark flopped back down on his face with his left arm sticking out at an awkward angle.

I stumbled towards Michael and, in maybe the most athletic moment of my short life, tackled him to the ground. It really wasn't all that impressive, because he didn't fight back at all. He simply fell down under me and started to cry. The next thing I heard was a police officer telling everyone to get down. I was ahead of the game for once.

CHAPTER 18

The next few moments are still a blur. I remember being very confused as the officers ripped me off of Michael and violently slapped handcuffs on both of us. I had done nothing wrong, of course, but they didn't know that. The only thing they knew was that there was a gun in the room, and they didn't know who'd had it. As one of the officers drove his knee into my back, my head was turned towards Mr. Mark's lifeless body. A paramedic had flipped him over and was attempting to perform CPR on him. I knew it was useless, but you can't tell a paramedic that.

The officers now had everyone that was still near the scene of the drama, with the exception of Mrs. Montoya, on the ground and handcuffed. That included two of the Spanish speakers, me, and Michael. There were about eight other kids sitting in the corner with an officer watching over them. I had no idea where Colin and Anthony had run off to.

Eventually an officer come over to me, pulled me up into a seated position, and began asking me questions. They were exactly the type of questions one would expect in this situation. They wanted to know if I knew why Michael would do this, why I got involved, did I know about it beforehand, etc. I answered as truthfully as I could with my mind as messed up as it was at the moment. I have no idea if I made any sense or not, but it was enough to get him to stop asking me questions and walk me over to the cafeteria wall, where I was told to sit until I was ready to be let go.

Michael wasn't treated so well. Mrs. Montoya led the police towards him and pointed. Three cops jerked him to his feet by his armpits and dragged him out through the emergency exit of the cafeteria. I wondered if I would ever see him again, other than on TV.

I was walked to the main office, uncuffed,

and asked to sit while they called my house. Ms. Linda, our head secretary, was shaking so badly that she could barely dial my number. "Ms. Hefler, there has been an incident at the school this morning. Yes, Max is okay, but you are going to need to pick him up as soon as you can. Yes, ma'am. No, ma'am. I can't discuss it now, ma'am. Okay. He's in the office. Thank you." She hung up, then looked back at her computer and picked up the phone again. There were eight more kids in the office waiting to have their parents called. Ms. Linda was in for a long afternoon.

Ms. Linda dropped the phone and put her hands over her face. She looked back up at me and said, "Son, you are bleeding. Take this." She held out a tissue for me and pointed at my face. I touched the corner of my mouth and felt wetness that I hadn't even realized was there until she pointed it out. I took the tissue from her and dabbed at my face.

It took me a minute to remember exactly why I was bleeding. It was the gun. I'd had a gun in my mouth a few minutes ago, and walked away with only enough blood to soak a tissue.

Unbelievable. I know I should have considered myself lucky, but for some reason it just didn't feel that way.

I sat in the office for another forty-five minutes waiting for my mother. A paramedic stopped by to check on me a couple of times, but most of her attention was taken up by kids that were obviously handling this whole thing worse than I was. One girl was crying so hard that she seemed to stop breathing at times.

From where I was sitting, I could see the office door when my mom burst in, crying and looking around frantically. "Oh my God! Max! Are you okay, baby?" she asked as she knelt down in front of me and pulled my head to her chest. She began to cry even harder.

"I'm fine, Mom. I'm fine," I mumbled, and I started to cry myself. "Can we please just go home?"

"Of course, baby. We can do anything you want. Anything at all," Mom whispered to me as we rocked back in forth, holding each other. Her tears were beginning to soak my hair, and I could feel her heart beating through her chest.

We stood, and my mom nodded at Ms.

Linda and thanked her as she led me out of the office with her arm still around me. Once we got in the car she calmed down a little, and then started asking me a bunch of questions about what had happened. I couldn't answer them. I was numb. Just like on the way to school, but for a very different reason.

CHAPTER 19

I spent most of my time for the next month or so in my room when my mom was home. Of course, none of what had happened was her fault. I knew this, but I still didn't want to see her, or anybody else for that matter. When she left for work I would come out of my room and watch TV.

During one of these TV marathons I saw a newscast that said a thirteen-year-old student was being held on murder charges over a school shooting. They couldn't use his name because he was a minor, but there was no doubt that it was Michael. They had a couple of different adults that I had never seen before talking about the shooting and what they thought was going to happen next. The legal analyst seemed to think that Michael would most likely be sentenced to a "mental health facility" because of his age. Fancy words for the nuthouse.

Lincoln Middle School was shut down for the next week as they tried to sort through the mess and assure parents that their babies were safe. I stayed home for almost another month afterwards. I couldn't even bring myself to go to Mr. Mark's funeral, even though I knew that I should. I just wasn't ready for that. Not yet.

After the funeral Colin stopped by my house. It was as awkward as you'd expect it to be. The doorbell rang and I opened up our apartment door to see him standing there wearing a dirty white dress shirt, a pair of jeans, and a clip-on tie. He looked very nervous as he fidgeted with his tie and hair.

"Hey, Max. How ya doin'?" asked Colin.

"Hi, Colin. All right, I guess," I replied as we stood in the doorway.

"You coming back to school?" he asked.

"Yeah, probably," I answered.

"Good. Hey. Thanks for helping me the other day," Colin blurted, like someone having a gun stuck in their mouth to help you out was the equivalent of passing the salt at the dinner table.

"Yeah, that was crazy."

"Yeah, it was. Okay. See you at school?" Colin said. He stood there looking at me like he was waiting for me to say something else. I could tell that he desperately wanted to talk about what happened. After a couple of moments of nothing, he said, "See ya," one more time and turned and headed back down the stairs.

Exciting stuff, I know, but really pretty typical for a couple of fourteen-year-old boys. We talk about our feelings about as well as fish climb trees. Part of me really did want to talk about it with him, yet I just couldn't make myself do it. Even though Colin and I were in a better place than we were before, I still didn't trust him completely. Hell, I didn't trust my own mother enough to have that conversation yet. I did appreciate the effort though. I knew he appreciated what I had done for him, because he wouldn't have come to my house in a million years otherwise.

A few days after the funeral the school starting sending over a social worker to talk to me about what had happened. I can't remember her name, and to tell you the truth, I was kind of rude to her. I just didn't feel like talking about the worst experience of my life to a complete stranger. I mostly just ignored her until, during her third or fourth visit, she stood up, sighed deeply, and left. The school called my mom to inform her that they wouldn't be sending her back, but if I did decide that I wanted to talk to someone they would be waiting for me.

I figured I was really going to be left alone with my thoughts for little while. I figured wrong. Two days after the social worker quit on me, there was a knock on my door. Mom was in the shower, so I put down my video game controller and got up to answer it.

"I'm coming!" I hollered after about the fourth knock. I opened the door to find Mr. Davis, my English teacher, standing there.

"Hey, Max. Got a minute?" Mr. D asked.

I had not seen this one coming. I thought that the next step in all of this would be my mom deciding that she had enough and dragging my big butt back to school.

"Sure," I replied, "Come on in."

"Thanks, Max. Is there somewhere we can talk?"

I led Mr. Davis through our living room, down the hall, and into the kitchen. On the way I hollered to Mom that we had company so she wouldn't walk out of the shower with just a towel on, or worse. The only thing worse for a fourteen year-old boy than seeing your mother naked is having someone else see your mother naked.

"Who is it?" Mom hollered back.

"Mr. Davis. He wants to talk to me," I shouted as we walked.

"Oh! I'll be right out!" Mom answered with a little too much enthusiasm. She thought Mr. D was cute. She had said so after our last parent teacher conference. My mom doesn't say much quietly, and a couple of girls waiting outside the classroom heard her. She even used the phrase, "Hubba hubba," at one point. I wanted to hide in a locker.

Our apartment is pretty small, so the entire journey to the kitchen took about five seconds. I cleared some of our dishes off the table and directed him towards a chair. He sat, put his elbows on the table, folded his hands together, and smiled at me. I circled the table and sat on the opposite side.

I was glad to see Mr. D, and I was pretty sure I knew that he was there to talk me into coming back to school, but I was still kind of nervous. It's weird enough to run into a teacher outside of school at all, but to have one in your house — that's really freaky.

"How've you been? A lot of kids have been asking about you," Mr. D said while surveying his surroundings. I think he was a little nervous, too.

"I'm okay. I'm not ready to come back yet, though," I blurted.

"Good, because I'm not here to talk you into coming back. That's somebody else's job. I just wanted to make sure that you're okay," Mr. D said.

"Yeah, I'm good. Kind of bored. Could be worse."

"That's good to hear. Have you been doing the homework that your mom picked up?" asked Mr. D. The school had put together a bunch of assignments for me to complete because I'd missed so much school. The only subject I even attempted to do was Spanish for Ms. Castillo. A man has to have his priorities.

"I'm working on it," I replied.

"Cool. Call me if you need help with any of it."

"I will," I said, but knew I wouldn't. We both stared at the table for a second, letting the awkward silence of my empty promise pass.

"Colin said he dropped by to see you. That true?" asked Mr. D.

"Yeah. Didn't stay long though."

"I know. We talked. He's worried about you, and even seems a little grateful. Believe it or not, you may have succeeded in helping Colin Culler grow a conscience," Mr. D said with a chuckle. I just smiled a little and fidgeted with a salt shaker. "All right. I'll get out of your hair. Before I go, I do have one question though. Why haven't you come back yet?"

A few people had tried to talk me into coming back to school, but no one had asked me so directly why I didn't want to return. I think they just assumed that they knew why. I wasn't sure what to say. I stared down at my hands, trying to put how I was feeling into words. Mr. D didn't look like he was handling this emotional stuff any better than I was. He was looking directly at me, but he didn't seem to know what to do with his hands. He kept going from adjusting his collar to scratching his cheek to checking his pockets. I guess guys suck at talking about this kind of stuff at any age.

"The general opinion back at Lincoln is that you must be in shock, or scared something like that might happen again. I think that's a load of bull crap," Mr. D interjected.

"Why's that bull crap?" I asked, a little offended. Didn't I have the right to be in shock? Shouldn't I be a little scared? I'd had a gun in my mouth, for heaven's sake.

"It's crap because no one that acted as bravely as you did that day in the cafeteria would be scared to simply come back to school. I know it, and so do you. What's the real reason, Max?" Mr. D's face had hardened a bit when he asked this question. I had never seen him so serious.

"I...I...I...," I stuttered.

Mr. D reached across the table and tried to

grab my hand. It wasn't an aggressive grab. I think he was trying to comfort me, but I pulled my arm away and abruptly stood up, pushing my chair back.

"I'm sorry, Max. I don't want to upset you. I just wanted to—"

"It's my fault!" I interrupted. "I knew about Michael's sister. I knew that Colin's dad beat him. I knew all of this, and I didn't stop it! Mr. Mark is dead, and it's all because I didn't say something sooner!"

I collapsed back into my chair. My heart was beating in my temples. I could feel my shirt starting to stick to my back because I was now in a cold sweat. I felt a lot like I had in Mrs. Jacobs' room when I lost it. I could tell that some of what I said was news to Mr. D by his reaction. He'd probably heard rumors about Michael's motivation, but I wasn't surprised that he had no idea about Colin's situation.

"Max, none of this was your fault," Mr. D said, "and if you really believe that, then it's time for a wake-up call."

"It is my fault. If I had told Principal Montoya about how upset and sad Michael was, or if I had told Michael why Colin was the way he was, Mr. Mark might still be alive," I said.

"Max, if you wouldn't have done what you did that day, Michael and Colin would both be dead. I truly believe that. I also believe that Mr. Mark was a grown man that knew exactly what he was doing. The bottom line is that you aren't responsible for anyone's actions but your own. Nobody is. We just try to deal with stuff like this as best we can when we have to. That's exactly what you did," Mr. D said while pointing his finger directly at my chest. He was standing now, and started to circle the table towards me. I stood up and took a couple of steps back.

"But I didn't do enough! Nobody should have died!" I screamed.

"You're right. Nobody should have died. But someone did. Mr. Mark died trying to keep a kid from making the biggest mistake of his life. It didn't work out the way he had planned, obviously — or maybe it did, I don't know, but there is nothing that can be done about it now. In my mind, the real question is, "Did Mr. Mark die for nothing?" Because if you don't start living again, it sure as hell feels like he did."

Just then my mom came into the kitchen, way overdressed and reeking of perfume. "Mr. Davis, what a surprise! Can I get you something to drink?" It was obvious that she was trying to turn on the charm. Gross.

"That's very kind of you, but I think I should be going," Mr. Davis said with a half-hearted smile.

I think my mom could sense the tension in the room. "Okay. Is everything all right?" she asked in a concerned voice as she looked back and forth between the two of us.

"Yeah, Mom. Everything is fine. I'll walk him out," I answered without taking my eyes off of Mr. D.

We made our way back through the apartment, out the front door, and onto the landing. I stood at the top and watched him make his way down the stairs. He opened the door and was about to leave when I stopped him.

"Mr. Davis, do you really believe that?" I asked.

"Believe what, Max?" he replied.

"That it wasn't my fault?"

"With all my heart. You know where to find me if you want to talk," he said as he closed the door behind him.

CHAPTER 20

Mr. Davis's visit got me thinking. He was right. I had to start doing something again. It was time to go back to school. As antisocial as I am, even I was starting to get a little lonely. Besides, I could tell I was starting to worry my mom way too much.

Even when I returned to school I was a zombie. It was just an exercise in moving from one room to another and then going home. I barely spoke. Some of the kids tried to start conversations with me, but it was pretty obvious that it was out of pity. I didn't want pity. I just want to be somewhere besides my room.

I wasn't really in shock any more, I just had some really crazy thoughts in my head, and I was afraid if I started to talk they would all just

138

come pouring out. For a while I wished Michael would have just shot Colin that day. I know, it's a horrible thought. But did Mr. Mark deserve to die any more than Colin did? I was sure he had a family somewhere that was missing him right now. Would Michael have shot anybody at all if Mr. Mark had never said anything to him? Would he have shot himself?

I continued to torture myself with unanswerable questions like this until a new piece of information gave me a whole new perspective on what had happened. I was waiting outside Mrs. Montoya's office to be called in for another one of our now weekly counselling sessions, when I heard two secretaries talking about Mr. Mark.

"Can you believe he never told anyone? To be that sick for that long and be able to keep it a secret. Mark was stronger than I am, that's for sure," one secretary said to the other.

I had no idea what they were talking about, but I had a feeling that it had something to do with what happened in the cafeteria based on their tone of voice. Whenever anyone at school talked about that day, their volume automatically dropped a hundred decibels and their voice got softer, as if they were going to wake a sleeping giant if they said it too loud.

My thoughts tended to direct themselves towards Mr. Mark quite a bit lately. I replayed the events from that day in the cafeteria every night; his words, the sound of the gunshot, those bloody hands. I couldn't stop thinking about those bloody hands.

"Excuse me, ma'am," I interrupted. "Are you talking about Mr. Mark?"

The two secretaries exchanged a concerned look. "Yes, we are, young man, but I'm not sure if we should...." The first secretary trailed off.

"I don't think it's any big secret anymore, Linda." She turned her attention to me and said, "Mr. Mark was very sick when he died. Cancer."

I had spent so many hours in my room trying to figure out why he had done what he did that day, but the idea that he could be sick had never crossed my mind. I felt like I had been hit by lightning. It all made sense to me now.

"Stomach cancer. Stage 4. I guess he didn't have much time left," she added.

I couldn't catch my breath. I stumbled out

of the office, pushing my way between two girls that were on their way in, causing them to drop their books.

"Young man, are you okay?" one of the secretaries hollered after me.

I didn't bother to answer. I had to get out of there to somewhere that I could think. I ran as fast as I could to the boys' restroom. I flung open a stall door and crashed down hard on the toilet inside.

I put a hand out to each side as if I was trying to push the stall walls out, and tried to catch my breath. Could it be true? Could he really have been dying anyways? I had sort of made my peace with most of the events of that day in October, but there was still one question I couldn't answer completely: Why did Mr. Mark confront an angry kid with a gun?

Now I knew. Yes, he was protecting us, but he knew he was going to die anyways, so he intentionally directed Michael's rage towards himself. He had been in pain for a long time, and had finally had enough. Enough of the cancer. Enough of the pain. Enough of everything. He could have easily stayed in his janitorial closet

141

until it was all over, but he didn't. In my mind, the ironic part was that he didn't die at the hand of one of those bullies. He died at the hand of one of the very kids he was trying to look out for in the first place. Who knows what might have happened to Michael, or Colin, if he hadn't been there that day? No doubt at least one of them would be dead—more than likely, both of them would be. Obviously he saved Colin, but in a way he saved Michael, too. Sure, he was probably going to spend a large chunk of his remaining years behind bars, but he was still alive.

I guess in the end Mr. Mark did what he had told me to do. His words echoed through my mind. "It do get better, but not until they know you'se had enough. They knows now."

CHAPTER 21

The news about Mr. Mark kind of snapped me out the funk I had been in since returning to school. I no longer wanted to waste away my days hiding in my room, either. If someone could be suffering as much as he was and still get up and go to work every day, then I had no excuse for staring at the TV and feeling sorry for myself under a mountain of Cheetos dust, or daydreaming my school days away.

A few days after the police concluded their very lengthy investigation, I opened the local newspaper to find an article about Mr. Mark. They called him a hero for distracting the gunman so that kids could escape. That wasn't exactly how it happened, but they definitely got the hero part right. Alongside the article they had reprinted his obituary. Since I was still in my dazed state when it came out the first time, this was my first chance to read it.

It turns out that his full name was Marcus Virgil Washington. He had been born in Baton Rouge, Louisiana in 1952. He married his high school sweetheart, Mildred, in 1971, and they moved to Michigan because he had gotten a job with General Motors at a factory in Detroit. They had three children—Jeffrey, Joshua, and Bernadette. I was glad to learn that he had such a happy family. However, the rest of the obituary wasn't as fuzzy and warm. It went on to say that his wife passed away from cancer in 1996, and that he lost one son as well, in 1984. According to the article, this boy, Jeffery, was only twelve when he died. It didn't mention how he passed away.

I read that last part several times, as if a deeper meaning would jump out at me if I just kept reading it over and over. I had to know how Jeffery died. Maybe it was because of my recent connection with Mr. Mark in the hallway, or the fact that Jeffery was about my age when he died, but I just had to find out. I had a feeling

144

deep in my gut—and that's saying something, ("Activate Comedy Shield….")—that the death of his son had something to do with how Mr. Mark acted in the cafeteria that day. The article didn't give any more information. I had some research to do.

CHAPTER 22

The library was about six blocks from my house, and I figured I'd start there. When a kid dies somebody must write a story about it, right? I walked up to the librarian's desk and waited patiently for the forty or fifty-year-old looking African American lady working there to help me. She was sorting books on a cart and, I think, testing my ability to wait at the same time. After about three full minutes she finally looked up.

"How can I help you, young man?" she asked with a slight southern accent.

"I am looking for old newspaper articles," I replied.

"Follow me, sugar. All the more recent newspapers you can find online now, but the older stuff will require us to fire up the old microfiche machine. Might have to dust it first," she said, as she gave me a wink over her shoulder.

She led me to the farthest corner of the library. She pointed to a table with a huge monitor on it that looked like it might have been from the world's first computer.

"What newspaper are you looking for?" she asked.

"Probably the *Detroit News* or *Free Press*," I answered.

"Which years?"

"Um, probably 1984 or '85," I said after glancing at the newspaper I had brought with me to check the date.

The librarian disappeared and came back several minutes later with an armful of what looked like sheets of plastic with dozens of tiny photographs printed on them. She set them down on the table next to me.

"There you go, sweetheart. Do you know how to use the...?" She stopped mid-sentence and pointed at the folded newspaper that I had set down next to the microfiche machine. "Did you know him?" she asked.

"Yeah. He was the custodian at my school. Nice guy. He died. I am trying to find out some more stuff about him. There was an article in the paper. It said he lost a son, but didn't say how it happened."

I looked up from the paper to see a very sad, concerned look on the librarian's face. Her bottom lip was trembling, and her eyes were in the beginning stages of a full-on cry. I wasn't sure what to do. I hate it when girls cry. I figured she was just sad for some random reason, like my mom is sometimes.

"Are you okay?" I whispered.

"Honey, we don't need this machine. I can tell you what you need to know. Marcus Washington was my father."

CHAPTER 23

I must have looked like a complete fool when I heard those words, because the librarian let out a little giggle and told me to close my mouth before I caught a fly. She wiped a couple of tears from her cheeks and asked me if I wouldn't mind moving this conversation back to the circulation desk, just in case anybody needed her help. Apparently this was going to take a while.

She told me that her name was Bernie (short for Bernadette) and asked me my name. I told her as we sat on two stools behind the monstrous mahogany desk. She pointed to a picture of five smiling people standing in front of a car. One person was an obviously younger, and surprisingly thinner, version of Mr. Mark. I

149

had this idea in my head that maybe he had been picked on for being fat when he was a kid, too, and that was why he helped me. Apparently not. It looked like his food issues came later in life. He was standing next to a very pretty woman wearing a blue sundress. She was holding a toddler that was probably four or five years old. Next to them was a boy that looked to be about twelve or thirteen, and another boy that was probably about seven or eight. It was as happy looking a family as I'd ever seen.

"That's one of the last pictures taken of all of us together. I think it was 1981 or '82. That's me in my momma's arms. Almost all my memories leading up to Jeffrey's death are happy ones," she said, before dabbing her eyes with a tissue and blowing her nose.

I desperately wanted to ask her how Jeffrey had died, but it didn't feel like the right time. I just sat and listened as she continued her story.

"Jeffery was my oldest brother. He was such a sweet boy. He'd get down on the floor with me and play for hours. Dolls even, if that's what I wanted to play. He was so handsome and funny." She was smiling from ear to ear as

150

she tilted her head to the side and ran a finger over the image of her brother. She seemed to get lost in her own memories for a second before clearing her throat, dabbing her eyes again, and sitting up straight. "Jeffery also had a severe speech impediment. Do you know what that means, dear?"

I had a pretty good idea, but I let her tell me anyways. I've learned when an adult asks you a question like that, they are going to tell you about it whether you want them to or not.

"It means he spoke with a very bad stutter. It used to frustrate him more than you could imagine. Sometimes he would just give up and not talk for days at a time—especially when the kids at school gave him a hard time. They were so mean to him. At least that's what he said in the letter Daddy found after he…." The words caught in her throat. She looked down at her hands, which were folded around a tissue in her lap. She continued to cry for several more seconds before looking back up at me through watery eyes. "It got to be so bad that Jeffery decided he couldn't take it no more. He killed himself, Max."

The conversation I'd had with Mr. Mark in his janitorial closet came rushing back to me. He really hadn't been talking about himself when he said he knew a boy once that should have stood up for himself. He was talking about his own son.

Bernie had returned her gaze to the tissue in her hand and started to quietly sob again. I didn't know what to say or do. Should I hug her? Should I say something? Finally I managed to gather up my courage enough to say, "I'm sorry."

"Thank you, sugar. It's been a long time — almost thirty years — but it still hurts like it was last Tuesday. I don't think I've talked about it in just about as long," she said as she collected herself again. "Daddy never talked about it at all, at least not in front of us kids. He was always a very private man. That's why I was a little shocked when I heard about what he did at your school. It's not like him to speak up like that."

"Did your brother ever tell anybody? About getting picked on, I mean," I asked.

"I know he told our folks. They went up to

the school for meetings a couple of times. The last time was because Jeffery had been skipping school to avoid the bullies. I think it was just too much for him. What I don't think Jeffrey understood was that by ending his life, he was putting everyone that loved him in even more pain. He wouldn't have done it if he knew. I believe that in my heart," Bernie answered.

"I get picked on a lot, too," I confessed, "for obvious reasons." I patted my belly, just in case she needed it spelled out for her. "Your dad and I had a talk the day he died. He told me I have to like myself before anyone else could like me. I think I kind of get what he was saying now. I never got a chance to thank him, for the advice or for saving us all at school that day."

Bernie looked at me through those watery eyes again and said, "Honey, I think he had the talk with you that he always wished he could have had with Jeffery. I'm sure those words have been on his mind longer than you've been alive. I have no doubt he found the courage to speak out to that boy with the gun because of it. Probably took a lot of weight off of his shoulders."

Great. Now I was crying, too. Bernie pulled me in for a hug, and we both cried like a couple of babies perched on those wooden stools. We stayed that way for a few minutes before pulling ourselves back together. I had one more question to ask before I left.

"Did you know about his cancer?" I asked.

"Heavens no. Like I said, Daddy was a very private man. I am sure he didn't want all of us crying and carrying on over him. Besides, I don't think that stomach cancer hurt him half as much as carrying around the pain of not being able to save his baby boy before it was too late. I think his actions that day allowed him to cure himself of something much worse than cancer. Regret. Thank you for helping him do that."

"I didn't do anything, ma'am," I said as I choked back my tears.

"Honey, you didn't have to do anything. You gave him a chance to make things better for someone, anyone. With all my heart, that's what I believe Daddy needed," she almost whispered as she pulled me in for one last hug.

I thanked Bernie for her time and left the library. Before I was gone she told me she would love to get together and talk more about her dad anytime I wanted to. I imagine that I will take her up on that someday. But before I could do that, I had one more person to talk to. I had to see Michael Dryden.

CHAPTER 24

"I still don't like this, Max," my mother said sternly from the driver's seat as she turned into the driveway of the psychiatric care facility. She stared straight ahead and gripped the steering wheel so hard that her knuckles had turned white.

I could completely understand why she felt that way, because I wasn't too excited about it either. Ever since I had spoken with Bernie, I'd felt as if I had to talk to Michael. I needed to put this whole thing behind me, and I didn't feel like I could do that until I spoke with him about what happened. It just felt like the right thing to do.

Mom pulled the car into a space about halfway across the parking lot from the building. The psychiatric institute was located in a one story, strip-mall looking building that housed other medical stuff like regular doctors, a chiropractor, and a massage therapist. It wasn't the nicest looking place. I guess if you're crazy and a criminal they don't exactly roll out the red carpet for you. I opened my door and started to step out of the car.

"You don't have to do this, Max. We can start the car and go right back home. You don't owe that boy anything. I'm worried about you being near him," she pleaded.

"It's okay, Mom. I'm sure they aren't going to lock us in a room and give him a weapon or anything. It's going to be fine," I said as I reached back, squeezed her arm, and closed the passenger side door. She'd offered to come with me into the building when we were getting ready to leave, but I refused. I wasn't sure what I was going to say to him, and having my mom there wouldn't be much help. I needed to do this alone.

I walked through the double doors and approached the reception desk. A nice lady slid back a glass pane and asked me how she could help.

"I am here to see Michael Dryden," I replied, trying to sound as old as I could. "I am a friend of his."

"One moment, please. I will check and see if he is able to have visitors today," she said as she swiveled her chair around and walked away from the window. I waited patiently for her to return, even though I already knew the answer. I had called his mother the day before to see if it was okay for me to talk to Michael. She was a little hesitant, saying that he really wasn't talking to anyone right now, even his lawyer, but I was welcome to try. She was also hard to understand. She kept dropping the phone and slurring her words. She wasn't taking all of this very well. What mother would?

Soon the receptionist returned to the window and said, "Doctor says it's fine. I will buzz you in. He's the third door on your left."

I thanked her and made my way over to a door on the opposite side of a waiting room. There was a loud buzz and a click. I opened the door and headed down the hall.

I'm not going to lie—I was more than a little

scared. This was a kid that had put a gun in my mouth a few weeks ago. I still haven't forgiven Julia McIntosh for stealing Doritos out of my lunch bag in fourth grade. This was a big step for me.

I found myself wishing that this hall was about a million times longer so I could get my thoughts straight in my head before entering Michael's room. I had rehearsed what I would say a few times since I decided that I was going to do this, but I was drawing a complete blank at the moment. I covered the forty feet of hallway a lot faster than I wanted to, and reached out to open the door. No turning back now.

I turned the knob, pushed the door open, and walked in. I was immediately taken back by the smell. It was like walking into the school locker room. The odors of sweat, stale food, and dirty clothing filled my nose. Michael still obviously wasn't very concerned about his personal hygiene.

The room looked just like anything you would find in a normal hospital. There was a large floor to ceiling curtain in front of me that I slowly swept to the side. Behind it was an adjustable bed, a sink, a table with what looked like an untouched lunch on it, and a television set on the wall. In the corner was a rocking chair that faced the window.

Michael stood up from the rocking chair and turned to look at me. He was so skinny that his clothes looked like hand-me-downs from a much older brother. His hair was disheveled and his eyes were bloodshot. From the expression on his face I could tell that he wasn't expecting me. I saw anger flash quickly across his face before his features softened and he seemed to relax.

"Max? What are you...? Why are you...?" he stuttered.

I didn't wait for him to finish his thought. I just went for it. "Mr. Mark wanted you to shoot him. He wanted to make sure you didn't hurt anyone else. He had cancer, Michael. Bad. He knew he was going to die, and he made you shoot him so that no kids would get hurt. He had a son that was bullied. Mr. Mark understood what you were going through." It all just kind of gushed out of me at once. I was afraid if I didn't get it all out at once that it might never be said.

Michael just stared at me. I had no idea if any of it had sunk in or not.

"I just wanted to let you know that," I said flatly as I turned back towards the door.

"I didn't want to shoot him. I didn't want to shoot anybody. I only wanted to scare Colin. I am so sorry," Michael nearly whispered as his words turned into tears and sobs. He laced his fingers behind his neck and hung his head. I turned and started to walk over towards him.

"No! Just leave. Please, Max. Just get out." Michael twisted his thin body around and slumped back into the chair and continued to cry. I waited a moment or two to see if he had anything else to say. When I was pretty sure he didn't, I turned for the door once again. Before I left, I did stop to tell him one more thing.

"Michael, I think he would have forgiven you. And I do, too."

CHAPTER 25

I didn't talk much on the way home. My mom tried getting me to tell her how things went, but I wasn't even sure myself. I didn't know if Michael had understood what I was trying to tell him or not. I just wanted him to understand that he wasn't alone, and that eventually things could and would get better. I wanted him to learn from Mr. Mark what I had learned from him—that it all starts inside of us, not with the bullies.

Sometimes I wanted to kick Michael's butt for putting us all through this, for putting a gun in my mouth, for what he did to Mr. Mark. Other times I wanted to give him a hug and tell him that he wasn't the only one that felt that way about getting picked on. Of course, I also wanted to tell him that violence wasn't the answer, but I think he already knew that now.

My visit to Michael wasn't all about him, though. I went to visit him for myself, too. I needed to stop thinking about the whole thing day and night. I wasn't getting much sleep and—drum roll, please—I had even lost some of my appetite. My clothes were getting a little baggy, and I could see a difference in my face when I looked in the mirror. I know this isn't the way I should be losing weight, but it was a start. My plan was to improve my mood while continuing to shrink my pant size.

I also had one more reason for seeing Michael. I never did get to thank Mr. Mark for the pep talk after my meltdown in math class, or for doing what he did in the cafeteria. If it wasn't for him I may have lost it, just like Michael. He could have easily ignored me and gone about his business, but he didn't. He wasn't exactly a knight in shining armor swooping in on his stallion to rescue me. No, what he did for me was more than that. He gave me the courage to rescue myself, from myself. My real problem wasn't Colin, or Anthony, or any of the other dozen bullies in my school. My real problem was the fact that I let myself be treated that way. Mr. Mark was completely right. I was going to have to start liking myself before anyone else ever would.

AUTHOR'S NOTE

I am currently a seventh grade English teacher in Bay City, Michigan. I am married to a beautiful woman who is also the mother of my two amazing daughters, but growing up, I was Max Hefler.

When I was fourteen I was an overweight, socially awkward, pimple faced kid that hated going to school. I would spend my days dodging from class to class, hoping not to have to talk to anyone about anything. I avoided teachers, I avoided students, I avoided everyone. I hated myself. In my own mind I couldn't come up with a single positive thing to say about myself, so I figured, how could anyone else possibly have anything nice to say about me? Because of this attitude I spent the majority of my middle school years locked inside my own head. I grabbed onto the negative and held onto it as tightly as I could, because it had become familiar. I knew how to be miserable, and I was good at it. Trying to make friends or be happy in any way was uncharted territory for me. The idea of stepping outside of this comfort zone was terrifying.

Now don't get me wrong—my entire childhood wasn't miserable. I was a perfectly happy kid for most of elementary school. Things didn't start to go south until around fifth grade. That was when kids started to notice that I wore the same clothes over and over again. That's when kids started to notice that my belly hung over the front of my pants when I sat down. Those things had been true for most of my life. What had changed was how other people responded to them. I was called every possible name you can think of. If a person hears something enough, they start to believe it. I went from being perfectly normal and happy to questioning everything about myself.

Thankfully, unlike Max, I had, and still have, an amazing mother and father. We never really had any movie-type moments where I poured my heart out to them about what I was going through and then they gave me some profound speech about being myself. Those things rarely happen in real life.

No, my dad saved me from becoming a "Michael." He did it by simply being there and spending time with me. He would come home from a ten hour shift at the factory he worked at and take me to the ball field to hit fly balls and play catch. He would take me up to his grandfather's land in Luzerne, Michigan, and we'd hunt or just walk through the woods for hours talking about baseball, home, nature, everything but the negative. Sometimes we didn't talk at all. During those days with my dad I would completely forget about my weight, the name calling, and all the other stuff that dominated my thoughts most of the time. Just the fact that he wanted to be with me, when he could be doing anything else in the world, spoke volumes. In those moments, that mean much more to me now than they did then, I learned a couple of valuable lessons. First, I learned that if you are going to live a full life there is no room or time for self pity. Life isn't about avoiding the negative; it's about finding the positive. The second lesson was probably the most important: I was worth someone else's time and attention.

I had some Mr. Marks in my life, too. These were some of my teachers, coaches, grandparents, and neighbors. I would not have grown up to be the person I am today if not for the direction, advice, and occasional kick in the pants I received from these people. At times I hated some of them for telling me things that I didn't want to hear. It took me a few years to realize just how much effort and care they put into me as I was growing up. They saw something in me that I couldn't see in myself.

Now, as a middle school teacher, I see dozens of "Maxs" walking the hall every day. I know who they are because they rarely make eye contact, almost never speak in class, and hate being singled out even for good things. I am sure you see them, too—or maybe you are a Max yourself. If you are, I just want you to know that things do get better. You are nowhere near the person that you are meant to be yet. You have so much growing and changing to do that five years from now you are going to look back and not even recognize the kid you are today.

If you see a "Max" in your school or neighborhood, don't let them feel invisible. Talk to them, wave, just smile, but do something. Anything. The joy that brief gesture can bring can change someone's entire day, month, even their life. If you are a "Max," it's time to start finding the good in you so that you can show it to the rest of the world.

MH; April 2015

About the Author

Matthew Hemingway was born and raised in Bay City, Michigan, where he has been teaching middle school reading and writing skills for the past 17 years. He earned his teaching degree at Saginaw Valley State University, where he also completed his Master's Degree in Educational Leadership. Along with teaching, Matthew has spent many years coaching high school football and wrestling as part of his educational career.

When not teaching, Matthew enjoys camping, hiking, and biking with his two daughters, Katelyn and Claire, and his wife of 13 years, Janelle.

Made in the USA
Monee, IL
24 January 2020

20803114R00099